The Crush That Crushed Me

Stocky Bonzz

<u>Dedication</u>

I dedicate this book to love. First love, new love, lost love, true love.
Whatever form of love this book finds you in...go for it and embrace it
but just don't let love blind you to what love is not.

Table of Contents

Intro...

Her rumbling moan sounded like she was purring in my ear, as I slow stroked her phat pink plum juicy lips. Those long slow in and out motions made me feel so high; especially by how much she was orgasming all over my mandingo. I kissed her neck; gently at first. Then I sucked on it hard, leaving a constant tingle traveling up and down her spinal. She liked a little pain mixed with a lot of passionate pleasure.

"Mmmmmmmm." She moaned. "Don't stop Ty."

"I got you baby. Just keep cumming for me." I whispered into the side of her neck, next to her right ear, as I felt all of her juices pouring out from her magnificent fruit garden, coating every inch of my long strong shaft. I couldn't stop, not even if I wanted to. She was rubbing my back, letting her nails lightly graze my skin and pressing her soft lips on my neck and shoulders. I didn't want to even think about the struggle of pulling out from her warm canal.

I pushed myself as far inside of her as I could go. She squeezed her legs like an anaconda around my waist, so I held myself firmly there. My rod throbbed repeatedly inside her. When I finally started stroking her again, she whispered, "Oh, baby. Haces que mi cono se sienta tan bien." {You make my poon-poon feel so good.}

"Asi Asi {Oh yeah, Oh yeah} I know I do baby, I got you so wet right now..." I fiercely said back to her. She felt like a human version of Niagara Falls, how wet she was. I slipped my forearms under her thighs and pulled her legs up onto my shoulders. Her water load of wetness was about to make my creme rise to the top. I felt like a volcano trying to hold back as much as I could from erupting. "I love you so much Tyrone my love, Te amo mucho mi amor Tyrone" she uttered out with much passion in her voice. I just wanted to last long enough to make her orgasm just one last time. So, I stroked her a little faster and banged my body into hers a lot harder. Our love making was getting so intense that it had the bed soaking and drenched. I wanted to let her know the feeling of my love for her was very mutual… even if I never said it out loud, she can feel it through all of my strokes. She put her hand on my stomach to try and slow me down, but I quickly snatched her hands, put them both above her head and held them there tightly. The look on her face said "give it to me papi", which told me that I was in the exact right spot I needed to be in, so I applied more pressure until her full juicy pink lips formed the perfect "O".

"Arrhh." I roared arrogantly like a lion claiming his throne as King of the jungle. "You like that baby, is it good to you? Tell me you want more; tell me you want it all!?"
"Y---ye----yesss." She stuttered. "It's so good. Give it all to me Ty!! Sigue acariciándome así!!" {Keep stroking me just like that!!}

I looked down into her eyes and kissed her luscious lips. I let my tongue roll around inside of her mouth and when I pulled away gently, she kept sucking on the tip of my tongue. I loved when she did that and she knew it too. I loved grabbing her chin and easing my thumb in and out of her mouth to suck on like a lollipop as well. I felt myself getting harder and I knew I was on my way to climaxing, on my way to pure ecstasy. At this point it felt like the earth was shaking.

I stroked even faster and much more harder and she held my neck with both hands firmly. I gave into her grip she had on me and I wrapped my arms around her back, hugging her tightly, as her legs began to shake. Right as I felt my own climax approaching, I heard a loud noise…

BEEP! BEEP! BEEP! BEEP! My eyes shot open. I jumped up out of my sleep. Swinging my feet to the floor, sitting up on the side of my bed. I put my head in the palms of my hands and said to myself, "Damn, another dream about her." I couldn't get her out of my head nor keep her off my mind, not even when I was sound asleep. It's crazy how we think we let go of old flames but love has a way of holding on somehow.

Chapter 1

How I met Joe *(My Big Brother)*

Joe invited me to a BBQ his new girlfriend Sariah's family was having at their house. That's where I first saw her, the love of my life, my childhood crush… but we'll get back to that in just a moment. Joe was my Dominican best friend/big Brother; although he wasn't my biological brother, he and his family sure treated me as such. It's crazy how Joe and I first met. It's the funniest story you'll ever hear in your life, peep.

When we were younger, we both went to the same elementary school, PS.23 in Jersey City New Jersey. Joe was in the 8th grade and I was in the 5th grade at the time; he was three years older than I was. Anyway, I wasn't that bad of a kid; [Yes, I was] but I always got myself in some type of trouble in school. Still, the teachers loved me because I used to rap, sing, dance and participate acting in a lot of plays the school was always preparing. My peers loved me because I would most of the time play funny characters that made all of the other students in the audience laugh so hard. I was a very exciting and hyperactive type of kid; but sometimes I'd be doing too much and some of the teachers didn't know what to do with me when I got to be too overwhelming for them to handle. Joe and I had classes right across the Hall from one another and what's so crazy about that is, we used to live right across the street from each other as well, lol crazy right.

My 5th grade teacher's name was Mrs. DeLuca, she was cool but kind of scary looking with the long-extended nails and all. She reminded me of one of the singers from the R&B group "SWV". The only difference was, she was Italian with long blond curly hair and drank a lot of cappuccino from Dunkin donuts. Mrs. DeLuca was one of those teachers that loved me but didn't know what to do with me when I started to act up in class. So, instead of getting me all the way in trouble by sending me to the principal's office to get suspended, she would take me out of her class and bring me over to Joe's bilingual teacher's class right across the hall. Mrs. DeLuca would ask Joe's bilingual teacher to let me sit in there to cool down for a little bit. Joe's bilingual teacher name was Ms. Weiss. She played the piano very well and taught the bilingual students proper English. I loved Ms. Weiss; she always had a smile on her face when Mrs. DeLuca would bring me to her classroom. She loved teaching me how to play the piano and she would always tell me I was a special kid.

I wasn't cool with any of the bilingual students just yet. They would always giggle at me and speak in Spanish about me every time Mrs. Deluca brought me to their classroom. I knew they were making fun of me, but I didn't really care because Ms. Weiss would always tell me to come sit next to her and learn how to play the piano. I was fine with that because it was fun to me.

One school morning, the principal put together an assembly for all the bilingual students in the school. They were all to report to the auditorium. I happen to be in Ms. Weiss' class at the time of the announcement about the assembly was made. As all the bilingual students were exiting the classroom to go to the auditorium, Ms. Weiss gave me the option to either stay in the classroom and do a piano lesson assignment on paper or go to the auditorium with them to watch the assembly. I chose to stay in the class and do the piano lesson assignment because I didn't want to go to an assembly that I wasn't going to be able to understand. Ms. Weiss told me not to leave the classroom until she got back or she would be in BIG trouble for leaving me unattended. *Yeah, she trusted me that much.* The last thing I wanted to do was get Ms. Weiss in trouble; but there was one problem. I had to use the bathroom bad as ever and the bathroom was outside of the classroom, all the way down the opposite end of the hall.

I thought to myself, *I can make it down there and back quick enough to be back at my desk before anyone finds out I'm even in here.* I went for it; running and ducking down from the door windows of each classroom I had to pass, I felt like an army soldier at war, ducking behind bushes taking cove. I made it to the bathroom and back to Ms. Weiss' classroom without being seen by anyone. *Yes!!* I celebrated in my head as I entered back into Ms. Weiss' classroom quietly. I made sure not to alarm any of the other teachers that were still teaching regular math and home economic classes. Teachers like my real teacher, Mrs. DeLuca, who were not at the assembly. I entered back into Ms. Weiss's classroom and closed the door very gently. I was back in the classroom by myself, safe and sound, *or so I thought.* I started to hear little noises and whispering voices coming from inside of the coat room closet; the closet of the classroom that I was in. I didn't really know what or who it was at first and I'm not going to front, I was a little nervous to find out. I was only 10-years-old at the time; but I was so curious to know who would be in that closet when I knew Ms. Weiss had left me in that classroom all alone. I started to tiptoe towards the closet and the noises got a little louder. Then I heard some giggling. It was bubbly, like the giggles I would get when Mrs. DeLuca brought me into Ms. Weiss classroom for being bad. I ducked down by the closet door, feeling like a spy in an action movie at this point. As I inched myself up, I took a peek into the glass window on the coat room door. As my eyes scanned the tiny room, I heard a girl say something in Spanish like "Si, cállate la boca" which means "Yes, shut your mouth" in English. The giggles got intense and not only did I hear girl voices, I heard guys voices as well. "Callate eres el que hace todo el ruido." (You be quiet. You're the one making all of the noise). At this point, I wanted to know who was in that closet and I wanted in on the action too. So, I burst open the door and scared the hell out of all four of them! "AHA!! Got Y'all!" I yelled out. "What are y'all all doing in here?" I asked; looking at the two girls who were in their bras with their shirts over their heads. I gave them my best interrogation stare, like I was the principal with a serious face. The girls didn't have a response for me because they didn't know too much English and looked pretty scared that I caught them doing what they were doing. One of the girl's mouths opened wide like when a snake is feeding itself, while the other girl covered her face. I couldn't peel my eyes from their chests. I stared for what had to be a full minute.

That was when one of the guys came up to me saying, "Oh shit, Oh shit. I'm sorry man, I'm sorry, bro; please don't tell Ms. Weiss." He was pleading with me.

I asked the guy, "Why shouldn't I?"

The guy looked at me and then looked at the two girls who were now covering up their chests. Then he walked over to me and asked, "Well, do you like what you see?"

I was like, "HELL YEAH! I LOVE WHAT I SEE!!" I couldn't believe he had to ask.

He then proceeded to ask me, "If the girls let you touch their melons, then can you not tell Ms. Weiss on us?"

I said back to him, "It's a f--king deal! I won't tell on y'all; you got my word!" So, it was an official agreement between all of us, including the girls. They let me touch their mangoes and even gave me a kiss too. I was satisfied, I never told on them.

A whole week went by before I was sent back to Ms. Weiss' class again. For some strange reason, I didn't hear any giggles from the bilingual students or no talks in their language about me when I entered the classroom this time around. I thought to myself, *that's strange*, but didn't really pay it any mind. All I saw were smiles on their faces; a few of them even waved hello to me.

Ms. Weiss was a little too busy that day to give me piano lessons, so she gave me an English assignment to do at my desk. The guy that I had caught in the closet with the two girls came to sit next to me at my desk. He said to me, "Hey, lil bro. I just wanted to come and thank you for not getting us in trouble last week."

I said back to him, "No sweat, bro. Y'all are all cool with me for letting what happened go down the way it did."

"It's all good." He smiled. "Hey, what's your name, lil bro?"

"Tyrone." I told him.

"What's up, Tyrone? My name is Joe and I'm going to make you my official little brother. Is that cool with you, Tyrone?" He extended his hand.

I slapped my hand into his. "Yeah, that's cool. I have an older stepbrother but he lives all the way in the Bronx; and I don't get to see him as often as I'd like to. I always wanted a big brother that lives closer to me."

Joe said back to me confidently, "Well, now you have one, me! Where do you live, Tyrone?"

I replied, "I live on Glenwood Avenue. Right across the street from a graveyard that splits two different projects. Marion Gardens and Dunking projects that is."

Joe's smile grew wider. "Oh wow! I do too! I live on the same block you live on. We could walk home and to school together now too, my new lil bro, hahaaaa." He hung his arm over my shoulder.

"That's dope!" I said excitedly as we walked off together.

That was how I first met Joe and became his brother/best friend. We've been close ever since and that is just one of the many crazy memories we share.

Chapter 2

When I first met Carmella/BBQ

It was a beautiful hot summer day on the 4th of July in the year 1998. I had just past the 10th grade and Joe had just finished his first year of college. We had just celebrated Joe's birthday the day before which was July the 3rd and we were planning on celebrating mine the very next week on July the 12th. I know what you're thinking, Yes, Joe and I also shared the same birth month. How ironic is that, right? Yeah, God knew what he was doing when he connected Joe and I together to be friends and/brothers. We had so much in common like we both loved playing basketball, Michael Jordan was both of our favorite basketball player in the NBA as well. Both of our favorite numbers were 7 and 23; we both loved listening to hip hop, reggae, salsa, merengue and especially bachata music; we both loved pretty girls and we both believed in God.

My parents and I moved out of Jersey City New Jersey and into the Capitol of New Jersey, Trenton. This was around my 8th grade year in 1996. I was pissed and heartbroken because I didn't get to graduate with the kids, I went to school with for seven whole years; and also, I was moving away from my best friend. I was really sad my 8th grade year in Trenton because I had to go to a whole new school and didn't know any of the kids there… not even one. It was like starting a whole new life for me; but it taught me something very valuable that I used later on in life. If you ever needed a new start at life, change your surroundings and relocate from the environment that you're known in.

I was very rebellious at first because I missed my old school. I missed living in Jersey City with the rest of my family/friends and I missed hanging with my best friend/Big Brother, Joe. That summer in Trenton, after graduating 8th grade, was terrible for me. I just couldn't adjust. I felt alone and uncomfortable more often than not. Even though Joe and I kept in touch over the phone like every other day, it still felt like we were far away from each other. Little did I know, that would all change soon.

After my 9th grade year in high school, Joe's parents offered me to go to the Dominican Republic with them again for the first month of the summer and also asked my mom if it was okay with her for them to take me with them to DR. This was the second time they were taking me to Dominican Republic with them. They wanted me to stay at their house for the whole summer. I begged my mom to say "yes" and she did. I was so excited that my mother had agreed and that ended up being basically what I did every summer of my high school years; but it was the summer after passing the 10th grade that I first saw her. She walked up from the alley way beside the house. Her almond eyes caught mine and it was like nothing else mattered. Like time slowed down just so I could get a good look at her, so that's what I did. I let my eyes roam from her brown eyes to her full voluptuous lips and then to the smooth, tan, sun-kissed strip of skin on her belly. Her half shirt hugged her breasts almost as tightly as her jean shorts hugged her hips and by the time she walked pass me, giving me a view of the rest of herself, there was no hope left for me. She was the love of my life. Her name was Carmella and I was crushing on her at first sight. I mean, I was head-over-heels for this girl, I had it out bad as ever to be with her. My heart raced, my palms got sweaty, my pants…. well…let's just say I was sure this was what people meant when they told their close friend "It was love at first sight". So, remember in the very beginning of this story, I told you Joe's girlfriend Sariah's family was having a BBQ that we were invited to, right? Well, that's where I first laid my crushing eyes on Carmella and immediately fell in love with her.

Joe and I had just arrived at Sariah's family's house. All you heard was loud Spanish music playing and a lot of fireworks going off on the outside because it was the 4th of July, Independence Day. Joe rung the bell rapidly... ring, ringg, ringgg---ringggg! Before we got there, Joe had been telling me about Sariah's fine-looking Dominican cousins because he wanted me to hook up with one of them, so we could all be one big happy family. That was always the plan; even before I ever met or even laid my eyes on anyone of Sariah's cousins. Joe told me there were like 100 cousins, but he knew that I was going to like Sariah's younger cousin named Carmella. What can I say? My brother knew me very well. Anyway, nobody was coming to the door, they must not have heard the doorbell ringing because of all the loud music that was playing and all the fireworks that were going off. We heard a lot of people in the backyard, so Joe decided to take us through the alleyway that led directly to the backyard. We finally reached a gate that lets you into the backyard and all I started to hear was "Joe Joee Joeee, Ven!!" Ven means 'Come' in Spanish. I mean, everybody back there was cheering for Joe. I saw that my brother was very famous over at this place and I was loving it. Sariah came up to Joe, gave him a kiss and grabbed both of us by the hand. She began introducing me to all of her family. Aunts, uncles, grandparents, guy cousins and those fine ass Dominican girl cousins Joe was always telling me about. I met them all; except for the one I was so eager to meet. I was frustrated because I really wanted to see her, even though all of the rest of Sariah's cousins looked gorgeous, I wanted to meet Carmella.

Sariah asked Joe and I, if we wanted her to fix us a plate of food to eat. We both looked over to the food, then looked at each other and back at Sariah and said "HELL YEAH!!" We loved to eat, especially if the food looked like it was going to be really good. The smell of the Spanish food was all in the air but it looked like it tastes way better than it even smelled. Neither of us could have turned those plates down if it would have saved our lives.

Standing in the middle of a party filled with beautiful girls, eating the banging plate of food Sariah had just brought us, Joe asked me, "Are you enjoying yourself bro? You good?"

"Oh, most definitely, my brother. These people are mad cool and very fun to be around." I responded while chewing my food.

"For real; they are." He reassured me." Yo… so, what do you think about Sariah's fine ass cousins? They are baddd, right?" Joe asked with a smile taking over his face.

"Hell yeah, man! They baddd as hell yo; but where is she at man?" I asked.

"Who? Carmella? I don't know, man. I asked Sariah and she said she doesn't know either; but she is supposed to be here. That's Carmella mom Angelina right there with her older twin sisters **Luzelena and Luziana**; and that's her younger sister her mom is dancing with right now. Her name is Maritza; she is nice too, huh?" Joe bragged.

"Yes, she is. they all are gorgeous; but I'm anxious to see Carmella because of the way you described her to me. I know she's the real bad one, I really hope she shows up man." I just knew the girl I had seen leaving was the girl for me and she had to be this Carmella girl too because she was fine as ever. As soon as I said that, I heard loud cheers coming from the crowd in the same backyard that we were all standing in.

"Weh! Weh! Wepah! Mella ta qui!" Which meant 'Mella is here' in English. I heard a soft voice from behind me say, "Excuse me, fellas." So, I turned around and seen those same beautiful brown eyes again from earlier. Carmella split right through Joe and I to enter the backyard. We parted out of her way with the plates of food in our hands, as she went to greet all of her family members that were at the BBQ. All I could see was her long beautiful wet curly hair, as it swayed gently just above her perfectly rounded ass. I was like a dog in heat, a raging bull that couldn't control my emotions. I was sweating bullets and all I could think was how badly I wanted her to be mine. Her legs looked firm like she ran track; they were as strong as horse legs. At the same time, the butter smooth tan creme color of her skin told me they had to also be soft. I wanted to touch them, to touch any and every part of her that she would let me touch. She had to feel me staring because I couldn't take my eyes off of her.

As she finished greeting her family, Sariah walked up to Carmella and started talking to her. I got a partial view of the side of her face. I don't know what they were talking about but they kept looking our way, sending Joe and I sweet smiles.

"Yoooo, you see her? That's her right there, bro. That's Carmella, that's your f***** wife, man. hah hah!" My big brother must have been reading my damn mind. "-Oh shit! Tighten up, here they come, bro." He tapped my chest with the back of his hand. Sariah and Carmella were walking towards us and each step closer they took towards us, made my heart beat faster and faster. I was seeing her very clear now. When I say, I had never seen a girl even come close to this girl's beauty before in my life, I meant it. Well, other than my girlfriend named Precious back in Trenton, I meant it. Precious was fine as ever too, she had the skin tone of golden honey with the cutest dimples on her cheeks. Her smile lit up any room. I always thought she was Beyoncé's younger cousin or something. She was sweet and I loved her dearly but Carmella was on a whole other level to me at the time! Anyway, Carmella and Sariah had finally reached us and Sariah started to introduce Carmella to me.

"Babe, you already know Carmella…" Sariah said to Joe. Then she turned to me. "I wanted to introduce her to Tyrone. Ty, this is my beautiful cousin Carmella."

She extended her hand out to mine and I was nervous like I was in the NBA finals with seven seconds left on the shot clock and my team was counting on me to take the game winning shot. I didn't know what to do nor say to her. I swear, I was stuck in all her beauty and trapped deep into her eyes.

"Ty? Tyrone!" Sariah said, laughing.

"Bro, snap out of it." Joe said, shoving me gently with his arm.

I suddenly grabbed her hand wanting to kiss it. "Oh, my bad love. I was gone off all of your beauty for a second; but I'm back now. Nice to meet you, Carmella, Oh my God, you're so Gorgeous." I said to her.

She softly smiled and said back to me, "Thank you. Would you like something to drink, I'll bring it for you?"

I replied, "Yes, I would love something to drink, anything of your choice, thank you."

"You're welcome. We'll be right back." She replied back as she walked off with Sariah and in that instance, she turned her head back around to me and smiled with this "I like you" look in her eyes. I didn't know if it was just all in my head or not. Was she just being nice or was she really digging the kid already? All I kept saying to myself was, *I hope this girl doesn't think I'm a thirsty one but if she does, she can definitely quench my thirst any day.*

"Yo, you was stuck, bro. Ha, ha, ha! So, what do you think about her? She's fine as f--k, right? Joe asked me the silliest question he had ever asked me thus far in life.

"Man, I'm in love, bro. I love her already and she doesn't even know it." I confessed. I didn't care about anything else except Carmella after meeting and greeting her. I was on a mission.

"Well, she will know soon enough. That's going to be your wife, bro. Just watch." Joe said, always thinking several steps ahead.

"Thanks for bringing me here, man. I think you and Sariah just might have introduce me to my wife." I said.

"Anytime bro, I got you." Joe said back to me. We both looked over at the girls. "That's definitely going to be your wife." We both laughed.

The girls came back over to us, we kicked it and talked for a little while longer. Then we all danced to the Spanish music playing the rest of the night away in the backyard.

Chapter *3*

The next day/Something's Wrong

The very next day came, and it was a beautiful gracious Sunday morning. I was knocked out cold in a deep sleep from partying hard the night before and dreaming about how my life would be with Carmella as my wife. All of a sudden, I felt a fluffy pillow hit me across my head and a female's voice saying, "Wake up! Wake up, we have to go to church you guys. Wake up, you two night owls." My vision was blurry and I was still half asleep, not wanting to leave my new wife in my dream alone. I thought it was Carmella in my dreams telling me to wake up because we had to go to church to get married and I was ready to follow her ass all the way to the church. Then "WHAM" the pillow hit me across my head again. This time much harder, waking me fully up out of my sleep.

My eyes were now wide open, I saw who it was hitting Joe and I across our heads with the pillow, trying to wake us up to go to church. It was our sister Maria. She was Joe's younger sister, her and I were the same age but I treated her like my younger sister because she was a girl and we were very protective over her.

"Come on, you guys, get up and-go get dressed. We are going to be late for church." Maria stressed to us. Even though Joe's parents gave us a whole basement to ourselves downstairs, any time we partied hard outside we would always come home and go upstairs to Joe's parents place and fall asleep on the nice fluffy carpet on the floor, with the TV watching us.

"Come on, bro. Let's go downstairs and get ready to go to church." Joe said to me. Another thing Joe and I had in common was that we love to get dressed up and always look sharp when stepping outside anywhere we went.

We got dressed and went to church, had a great service and were on our way walking out of church service in no time. As we were walking out, the preacher stopped us at once. He dipped his finger into this little bottle full of Virgin oil and placed a cross on all of our foreheads. He said to us all, "God-bless you." We all said "Thank you, God bless you" back to the preacher and exited the church doors.

We walked Maria and their parents to their Mercedes Benz. They open their doors and hopped in the car but before pulling off, Joe's dad said to Joe in his very strong Dominican accent "Oh yeah, bring us back some comida{food} from Gusto Latino when ju are on jur way back home, sons, Okay?"

Joe replied, "Tato{Okay}." and they drove off.

Walking back to our Lexus, Joe and I immediately started conversing about the night before; since we hadn't gotten a chance to do so as of yet.

"Last night was the Bombbb, right bro! I saw Mella's mom grab you to dance with her and I also saw that look Mella gave to you when she was walking away about to go get us our drinks. I think she likes you, bro!" Joe said to me with a big smile on his face. When it came to girls, we were like a kid's in the candy shop and although I knew Joe was making things a little bigger than what they really were, the thought of it was very exciting for me. So, I played right along.

"Yeah bro, I saw that too; but she was just probably being nice to me. I don't know" I said… "but what I do know is that I can't get her out of my mind and I'm not mad at that at all. We have to figure out a way for me to see her again. I love that girl man!" It was a confession that rolled so easily off my tongue.

"Don't worry, we will figure something out and make sure that happens again, bro." Joe assured me. *Ring, Ring!* Joe's cell phone started to ring as I was just talking in the air about how much I really liked and wanted to see Carmella again. "Oh snap! Hold up, bro. It's Sariah calling me, let me answer this. "Hello? What's up Babe?" He answered his phone. "Whattt? For real? Oh damn, that's crazy yo! Okay, babe. I will try to get as much people as I can to go with us to help support him and the fam. I know I got Tyrone to go with us for sure so far. Okay babe. Ty and I are headed to Gusto Latino to pick up some food for my parents right now. I'll call you back as soon as we get home.... I love you too... okay bye." Joe ended the call and looked at me with a very sad look on his face.

"What's up, bro? Is everything alright?" I asked.

"No, man… it's not. I'll tell you everything when we get to Gusto Latino; we have to sit down and talk about this one." Joe responded.

"Okay." I said.

We pulled up right in front of the Gusto Latino restaurant and parked the Lexus right there. We got out and walked into the restaurant, ordered our two plates of food and three platters to go for Maria and Joe's parents. We sat down at one of the tables in the restaurant to eat our food; but before we ate, we said our prayers. After saying our prayers, we took our first bites into the delicious food.

"Mmmm, this food is always banging, yo" I said to Joe. As we were chewing our food, I looked at Joe eagerly, waiting for him to tell me what was going on with that phone call he had gotten earlier from Sariah. He didn't say anything, so I asked. "What's up, bro!? What's wrong, what's going on!? Is Sariah alright; what happened?" I asked Joe.

"Oh yeah, man. I was so hungry. I almost forgot to tell you what's going on. My bad man." He took another bite and chewed it before continuing.

"Mella is in trouble, bro! Well not necessarily her, but her father is in trouble. He's locked up right now." Joe responded before shoveling another spoon of food into his mouth.

My heart nearly dropped when he said Mella was in trouble; but I still felt bad because even though I didn't know her father. It was her Dad. "Whattt, how that happen? What do we have to do? How can we help, bro!? I asked Joe with deep concern in my voice.

"Well, I don't know the whole story as of yet; but remember Sariah and Mella's two boy cousins Sun-Sun and Dolla? We met them last night at their mom Benzy's house." He paused for confirmation and I nodded yes. "Well, it's something about Mella's pops was with Sun-Sun's pops and they got busted with some drugs by the cops. Mella's pops was there getting a ride home from work and Sun-Sun's pops had drugs in the car. Sun-Sun's pops is this big timer in New York and he told the cops that he didn't know where the drugs came from; Mella's pops is saying the same thing. So, they both got locked up. Sun-Sun's pops made bail; but not Mella's pops because he's illegal in the country. They are holding him and talking about giving him some jail time over here in America and then deporting him back to Dominican Republic. So, Sariah asked me to get as many people as I can to help support Carmella's father in his case and maybe the judge will be lenient on him. This is your chance to see Mella again. By showing up to support her and her family in such a difficult time, you'll definitely get some brownie points for doing so. She would definitely respect you and like you more for just even being there, bro. You have to go with us if you want any type of chance at making her your girlfriend, man." Joe went back to eating.

In slight shock after hearing the situation; but knowing he was right about this being my chance, I looked at Joe directly in his eyes and said, "You know I'm there regardless, bro." I wanted to be there for her and thought it was a well-executed strategy at getting closer to Carmella.

We finished up the rest of our food, paid for our food, left a healthy tip on the table, and walked out of Gusto Latino. We got into our car and Joe started to drive us back home. It was a quiet ride; all we had playing on the radio was our favorite Mobb Deep song "Dearly Departed". [Go search that song on YouTube now and play it at low volume on repeat, while reading the rest of this amazing book]. Whenever tough times came about, we didn't like to say too much to each other until one of us came up with a great solution to our problem. We would just play music from our favorite rap artists; Tupac, Notorious B.I.G, DMX, Wu-Tang Clan, Outkast, Goodie Mobb and Mobb Deep. We were into that mob type of lifestyle. We love the movies like "The Godfather", "Goodfellas", and "Scarface". All of those great HipHop artists just mentioned gave us the feeling that we were ready for anything in real life itself.

We pulled up to our house and Joe told me to hang tight in the car; he was just going to run the food upstairs to his parents and then we were going to go to his cousin Los' house to chill, talk and think things over. Not only was Los Joe's cousin, he was my childhood friend as well. Los had all the video games and board games you could ever think of. He also had a pool we used to always go swim in and a half court we used to play basketball on as well. We all used to always play in Los backyard every single day, that was our playground.

Los lived right next door to Sariah's aunt Benzy's house. Aunt Benzy's was the house Joe and I were at partying with Sariah, Carmella and the rest of their family that night. We pulled up to Los' house and parked the Lexus right in front of his house. We got out of the car and walked up to his house, opened up the screen door and walked right in. *We were allowed to walk in like that because we were family.*

As Joe and I walked into the house, the first room we saw to our left was Los' big brother Fritos room. We walked into his room and he was organizing his major collection of comic books. He had them all; every comic you could think of. "What's up, Frito?" Joe and I said at the same time.

"What's up, fellas?" Frito said back, as he continued to fix his comic book collection and play himself in the Battleship boardgame.

Joe and I left his room and proceeded to walk through the house until we found Los and our other good friend Macho playing NBA Live on the PlayStation. "Yo, what's up fellas? Who's winning?" Joe greeted them.

"Who else would be winning? What's up, Blak? How you, bro?" Macho responded.

"Yeah, just got some shit on my mind. Pause that game fellas, we gotta have a meeting. There's some serious stuff going on right now. It's tent talk time fellas." *"Tent talk time" was when all of us got together, snatched a few beers out of the refrigerator, grabbed a few bags of chips, grab the big boom Box and went to sit in the tent outside all the way in the back of Los' backyard to talk about serious situations going on in our lives.*

As we were all sitting in the tent listening to our favorite "Mobb Deep" song "Daily Departed" once again, Macho asked. "So, what's the deal, fellas? Is everything alright?"

Joe and I come out and explain the situation about what's going on with Carmella's father and how we can all help by going to the courthouse with her and her family to support them in the serious situation. We also explained to them who Carmella was and how much I liked her even though I had just met her.

"Damn, that's deep." Macho said.

"Yeah, that's crazy." Los said.

"Yeah, it is right? So, are y'all going to go with us or what? His court date is tomorrow in Newark at the courthouse? We are all meeting up at Journal Square Station to go take the train there?" I said.

"Damn, I wish we could, man; but Los and I start our new summer job tomorrow. You definitely have to go though, bro. That would be a good look in all types of ways if you are trying to get with this girl Carmella you're talking about." Macho replied.

"Word, you right, bro. I understand that y'all have to go to work and I know it's such short notice. We just found out ourselves." Joe added.

"If I knew in advance, I would have tried to get a good lawyer for her father and had the whole damn state in Newark New Jersey tomorrow. For real." I responded back to the fellas.

They laughed just a little at what I said but they all knew how serious I was. We sat there for a few more hours listening to the music, drinking Coronas, and talking about the girls we liked, the rest of the night out.

Chapter 4

Carmella fathers court case/The Verdict

Sariah, Joe, and I waited at Journal Square path train station to meet up with everyone else from Sariah's family that was going to the courthouse. The dollar van that came from downtown where Carmella family lived, pulled up to the bus stop at Journal Square. Angelina, who is Carmella mother, got off the van first with greetings of hugs and kisses on the cheek to each of us. Then Carmella's twin sisters Luzelena and Luziana proceeded to get off the van next. Carmella's younger sister Maritza got off next; and lastly but my soon-to-be wife, Carmella, got off the van with the saddest look on her face. I felt so hurt for her, I just wanted to hug her right away and tell her that everything was going to be okay… but I wasn't so sure it would be.

She looked so confused, but at the same time, very happy to see me there. She greeted me with a smile, a hug, and a kiss on the cheek. We all proceeded to walk down the escalator that took us to the path train. It was a busy Monday morning and the trains were packed; everybody was going back to work from the 4th of July weekend that had just passed.

Without any planning on my part, Carmella and I got stuck standing next to each other on the train, holding onto the same pole together. We were close enough that the sweet smell of her perfume danced under my nostrils. The train bumped us together and I knew she had felt the semi-bulge coming from the zipper part of my pants, I had been trying to get to go down the whole train ride. She blushed a little and brushed a single curl from her face before she said, "Hey Tyrone, thank you for coming with us; but I'm a little shocked to see that you're here. Do you know where we are all going?" She asked, looking up at me in a way that threatened my strength.

"Yes, I know all about what's going on, Mella. I'm very sorry to hear this about your dad and I'm here to support you and your family. Plus, I wanted to see your gorgeous face again." I confessed with a quick smile.

"Aww, that's so sweet. Well, I thank you for coming and I appreciate you being here Tyrone. It really means a lot to me." She flashed a weak smile back at me. "Anytime, my love." I said back, hoping like hell the "I want you so bad" feelings washing over me weren't showing on my face.

The train stopped at Newark Penn Station and we all got off. After making sure everybody was with us, we proceeded to walk towards the court house. It was the longest 10-minute walk I ever walked in my life because Carmella and I talked to each other the whole time. We learned so much about each other in such little time; it was amazing. I learned that she had a boyfriend name Lenny; but she said he treated her like shit and really didn't appreciate being with her at all. It was like good music to my ears because if her boyfriend wasn't treating her right, maybe she would give me a chance to do right by her. She learned that I was originally from Jersey City but moved to Trenton New Jersey to live with my parents and that I had a girlfriend named Precious out there as well.

"So, do you like this girl a lot or are y'all just starting off fresh?" She asked.

"It's pretty fresh but I do like her a lot. She's a very beautiful and nice girl but she might not be the one like I thought." I replied.

"Why is that?" She asked me with this look in her eyes like she already knew my answer. This was the second time I noticed this look in her eyes, I just hope my physical response wasn't just as obvious.

"Because… there's another girl out there that I just recently met. I know she's my wife; she just doesn't know it yet… or maybe she does. I don't know." We locked eyes and laughed lightly at what I said as if we both knew who this mysterious girl.

Still, Carmella asked, "Oh wow, what's her name? She sounds like an amazing girl already. Why don't you go after this girl you are telling me about? Just let her know how you feel about her."

I responded, "I can't tell you her name because you might know her. She's from Jersey City and lives right around where you live; but I will tell you this… in time, I will let her know all of my feelings. I know she'll fall in love with me because I'll always treat her how she deserves to be treated… like a Queen."

She said back, "I love your spirit and mind, Tyrone. If this is really who you are, I think any girl would love to be loved by you. Go after the one you love; she is probably waiting for you."

As we finally got to the court house, we all walked into the court room together as a family. We sat down on the bench chairs and waited for Carmella's father name to be called by the judge. I could tell everyone was very anxious, nervous, and worried all at the same time; but I didn't know how to feel.

"Franky Mendoza!" The judge finally called her father's name. The bailiff brought him out and the whole family started crying his name and yelling out to him. "Franky! Franky, Te amos! Papa! Mi amor, we love you!"

Carmella and her family continued to chant their support to her father after the judge ordered them to settle down. He just looked back at us and nodded his head as if he was saying to all of them, "Be strong and I love you back." He looked like a good man in a bad position. To me, he definitely didn't look like he belonged in those handcuffs. Of course, I wasn't the judge.

The judge started in on the case. "Mr. Mendoza, you are charged with ...." He read him all his charges and they were all pretty steep and major. He was going to need more than just a public defender to beat this type of case with all those serious charges attached to it. Carmella family didn't have that type of money to get a good lawyer at that time and the guy he got in trouble with in the first place, never came through on the promises of getting him the help he'd need to beat the case. Then the judge read the verdict "Mr. Mendoza, the court has found you guilty of all counts and I order that you serve the rest of your 3-year sentence out here in a maximum-security facility. After which, you will be transported to immigration, they will handle you from there. Good luck, sir." The judge banged his gavel and it all sounded so final.

All you heard was, "No, NO, NOOOO!" and loud cries from Carmella and her family. I comforted Carmella with a strong hug and rubs on her back. I felt so devastated for all of them, I could see how lost they each felt without him in that moment. As Carmella cried in my arms, I held her tight and told her everything was going to be alright. That she had to be strong for herself and her family more than ever before now. I also told her that I wasn't going anywhere. I had her back.

There was nothing but silence on the train ride back home. Everyone was distraught and shocked over the verdict. We got back to Journal Square twice as fast as we had got to Newark. Sariah, Joe and I walked Mella and her family back to the dollar van that would take them back to downtown Jersey City where they lived. Once again, Mella and I walked alone just a little behind everybody else, talking to each other.

She sniffled. "I can't believe they did that to my father. Fuck that judge!" Carmella yelled out. "I'm sorry Tyrone, I'm just so upset right now… and so hurt. I love my father and they just took him away from us!" She wiped away a tear and sniffled again.

I was just listening to her, letting her vent out everything as we continued to walk to the dollar Van. When she paused to gather herself, I stopped us both in our tracks, grabbed both of her arms, looked her deep into her teary eyes and said, "I feel you; I feel your pain so heavily right now and I'm so sorry this has happened to you, your family and mostly your father. Sometimes, life brings us rough roads to cross but we must find a way to pave that road because if not… we will continue to experience bumps of hurt, discomfort and difficulty as we're trying to cross it." I don't know where all that came from, but it was right on time.

She replied with a sniffle, "Damn Ty, that was so deep. I like that; it touched my heart. You're right; but the way you said it… that was like some real poetic stuff right there. Do you write poems?"

I responded with a slight smirk on my face. "Yea, I'm something like a poet; I write music." I could tell she was really interested in me at this point.

We were getting closer and closer to the dollar van and it dawned on me quickly that this might be my first opportunity to get her number. So, I asked her... "Mella, what's your cell phone number? We should keep in touch."

She replied back with a smile. "Oh okay. Yes, we should... but I don't have a cellphone right now. I'll be getting one soon though. For now, just take down my house number. It is (201)434-8967, call me anytime." She kissed my cheek right at the corner of my lips. It caught me completely off guard and before I could rebound from it, she was on the

Dollar van. I saw her and her mother through the window of the van. They sat down in their seats and she waved goodbye to me from her window seat.

Chapter 5

Visiting Carmella at her job

It was the first Monday in September and everyone was celebrating Labor Day all weekend. This would be the last weekend I'd spend in Jersey City before I had to go back home to Trenton to start my 11th grade year in high school. I was so pissed at myself because I haven't seen nor spoke to Carmella since she gave me her number and two weeks had already passed. I had been wanting to call her and go see her; but what was I going to say to her? I had a lot of doubt in my head at the time on whether she would pick up my calls or if she really even wanted to see me again. I was thinking that she probably didn't want to be around anybody because she had just lost her father to the prison system; so, I decided to give her some time and space to herself to adjust to her father's situation.

Ever since the last day I saw her waving goodbye to me out of the dollar van window, I had been wanted to speak to her every day so badly. She was all I could think about most days. I'm not going to lie though; I was a little nervous about calling her. This girl was like one of those exciting rollercoaster rides from Six Flags Great Adventure that made your stomach drop. You know you wanted to experience it so badly but the closer you got to the front of the line the more your nerves took over your body.

Joe and I wanted to have our own little BBQ with the rest of the fellas we were friends with. We called up Los and Macho to see if they wanted to join us. Of course, they said "Yes, let's make it happen". Los wanted us to come over to his place to have the BBQ being that Macho lived only two houses away from him and Joe and I were driving. We all agreed to meet at Los house and have the BBQ in his backyard. We could play basketball and play video games there as well, listen to music and go swimming if we chose to do so; all while the food was cooking on the grill... but first we had to stop at the supermarket to buy drinks, meat and hotdog buns.

Riding in the car, on our way to the supermarket, Joe asked me, "Yo Ty, have you called Mella yet?"

I shook my head as I answered. "Nah bro; I haven't and I don't know why. I want to; but I just don't know what to say to her right now. You know she just lost her father and all."

Joe responded, "Yeah, man. I know; but she was feeling you that day we went to court with her. You have to call her, man. At least just to say "hi" and ask her how has she been. You know what...forget calling. You're going to speak to her face to face!" He made a quick U-turn.

I said, "What!? where are we going!?"

"To her new job. She just got on at One State Supermarket. It's perfect because we have to pick up some stuff for the BBQ anyway. Don't worry about it; I'll go in with you, so it doesn't look awkward, you know." He assured me.

"Oh, for real? She has a new job at One State Supermarket? That's dope... Aight man cool, let's go then." I agreed.

Joe started trying to tell me the plan of how we were going to play everything off when we got to her job to see her; but I didn't hear a word he said because my head went into this trance thinking about seeing her again. My stomach kept curling on me, just thinking about what was about to happen, it put my nerves on edge. I was excited; but at the same time, I was nervous as ever.

As we were pulling into the big parking lot of One State Supermarket, my head started to come back to reality and all I heard was Joe saying, "She should be on the cash register; you got this, bro." He parked the car and we got out and walked up to the entrance doors of the supermarket.

As soon as we walked into the supermarket, we heard loud Spanish music playing throughout the entire market. We could see all the cashiers with their backs toward us, checking all the customers out. I spotted Carmella immediately because I knew her body frame from head to toe, front to back and boy was the view of her pleasant from the back. The first time I saw that round plumped ass of hers, I swore I was hit and killed by it because I was in heaven, hypnotized, and thanking the Lord he allowed me into the heavenly gates.

Anyway, Joe and I proceeded through the entrance doors and into the supermarket, grabbing an empty cart and walking down the first aisle to find the stuff we needed. We finally got everything we came for and were ready to check out. Carmella was on register seven and it was such a coincidence that she was because my favorite number was seven. When I saw that, I thought to myself, *either GOD is showing me a sign or my mind is just playing tricks on me.* Whichever one it was, I was more than find with it. I just couldn't shake my nervousness; but regardless I knew what I had to do.

There were two customers in front of us as we approached her register; it was very busy in there. I briefly wondered how many BBQs were about to happen. Standing in line, all I could think of was how gorgeous she looked swiping groceries across her register. Her hair was hanging down around her backside... curly and long and shining like she had just washed it in a jar full of gel or something. It seemed like every customer and employee she worked with knew her because she kept a cute smile on her face as she rung up the customer's items and was very quick at getting them out of the supermarket.

At this point, there was only one customer in front of us; but of course, they had a cart full of groceries. She turned to her right for a split second to see how long her line was and noticed that Joe and I were standing there. She was shocked but surprisingly happy to see me. Honestly, it was almost like she was very excited to see us. "Hey fellas!!" She shouted.

We both waved "Hello" to her with smiles on our faces and said back loudly, "What's up, Mella?!" Joe and I always gave others the impression that we were always excited about what was going on in our day when they saw us together because truthfully... we always did have something good going on. I mean we were the life of the party wherever we went.

As Carmella swiped the last item of the customer's groceries that was in front of us, she put their item in the bag and gave them their total. "Your total is $107.86, sir. Would you like to use cash or debit?"

It was like the customer just realized where he was and what he was doing there at this very moment because a surprised expression took over their face. "My God, I forget my card at home and I have no cash on me. I'm sorry but I can't buy any of this stuff." The customer said to Carmella and walked away in embarrassment.

Joe and I finally walked up with our cart, shaking our heads because we knew Mella had just rung all that stuff up for nothing.

"Hold on, guys. I have to clear all these items back out of my system because the guy forgot his money. Can you believe that? There's like a hundred items here and then I have to go put this stuff back before I go home too. Insane!" She said to us.

"Yeah, that's crazy. How you get all that stuff and don't even have no money on you to buy none of it? That is insane; but take your time, love. We're not in any rush." I said back to her in agreement and tried to make her feel better.

She looked pretty frustrated and it made me feel bad for her. *I never liked to see her sad or upset.* "Anyway, how y'all been? What do y'all have going on today?" She asked, as she hit keys on her register.

"It's Labor Day and Tyrone's last weekend here before he goes back to Trenton. So, we're throwing a little BBQ with some friends. You should come through when you get off." Joe let her know.

"Yeah, I wish I could; but looks like I won't be getting out of here until about 10:30 tonight and I'll more than likely be tired by then. Thank you for inviting me though." She shook her head as she continued to hit keys on her register. "So, how have you been Ty?" She looked up from her register and into my eyes.

I was so in shocked that she was asking me how I was doing, I almost choked on my own words responding back. I got it together quickly though. "I'm doing much better now that I'm seeing you again; but I should be asking you how have you been, love?" I asked her back in the smoothest tone I could manage. "I've been hanging in there. Still can't believe what happened to my father; but I'm dealing with it, you know." She responded as she started to ring our items up.

"Yeah, I know; everything is going to be okay. On another note, I wish you could have brought your gorgeous self to this BBQ we're having; but I understand." I flashed my winning smile.

"Yeah, me too. So, you go back up to Trenton soon, huh?" She asked me with a semi-sad expression on her face.

"Yeah, I have to leave some time tomorrow. I have school the day after that. Eleventh grade, here I come." I replied confidently.

"Oh wow, you'll be in the 11th grade and I'll be going to the 10th grade, that's pretty cool. Well, good luck, maybe we'll see each other when you come back to Jersey City again." She said, ringing up the last item in our cart.

"Thank you, love; and we will most definitely see each other again. You still have the same number you gave me, right?" I asked.

"What, my house number? Yes. $35.73." She said back to me, while telling us our total for the groceries.

"Here you go." I handed her two twenties. "Okay good, I'll give you a call when I'm back home in Trenton, so we can speak more... if that's alright with you." I said, staring into those deep brown glazing eyes.

"Thank you and yes, I would love for you to call me." She reached into her bag and took a picture out she had of herself and gave it to me. "This is for you to remember me by. Call me, Tyrone." I got lost in her eyes for a few more seconds. Joe nudged me on my side, snapping me out of my stare down. "Okay, cool. I most certainly will. Thank you. It was good seeing you again, Mella. This is your tip jar, right?" I asked, pointing to a jar with coins and singles in it. "Here's $20 for the last customer inconveniencing you." I flashed her another smile. "Enjoy the rest of your day and night, love." I said as Joe and I headed to the exit door of the supermarket with our cart full of groceries. Something told me to turn my head around and see if she was watching us walk out of the supermarket. So, I turned my head around and sure enough, she was looking at us. She waved goodbye to me and I waved goodbye back to her. I was mad hyped!

Chapter 6

The Call

My first day back at school, all I could think about was the last time I saw Carmella and her waving goodbye to me with that beautiful smile on her face. It kept playing through my mind all day; and even though I had a girlfriend at the time, all I could think about was Carmella. How I wished I hadn't let my nerves get the best of me; what that last two weeks could have been like, and what it might feel like to kiss those soft lips of hers.

School had just let out and it was a very cold day walking home that Monday afternoon in Trenton; but I was prepared for the weather. I used to walk home with my Dominican friend, Melvin and his sister Julinda. We used to go to his house after school and listen to all types of Spanish and hip-hop music, play videogames and talk about all the girls we liked. Sort of like how Joe and I would do when I lived in Jersey City. Melvin was in the 10th grade, I was in the 11th, and his sister was in the 12th. She was so fine too, that was another reason why I liked to hang out with Melvin. His sister Julinda reminded me of Carmella in a lot of ways and I knew she had a little crush on me as well; but we never pursued each other.

Anyway, I remember this very particular Monday like it was yesterday. We were chilling at Melvin's house and his sister put on some Spanish music, it was called Bachata and I loved it. I had already learned how to dance Bachata because of Joe's family. That's where I learned most of the Spanish culture and their music. When Julinda put the music on the radio, she put on a Dominican artist by the name of Raulin Rodriguez and the song title was "Dame Corazon" which meant "Give Me Your Heart" in English. She asked me to join her for a dance; this wasn't out of the ordinary because she always freely danced around us. Still, I was a little nervous at first because as I said before… she reminded me of Carmella. I thought to myself, *this is the perfect opportunity to practice my dance moves so that the next time I see Carmella, I will have the confidence to ask her to dance if there's some Spanish music playing.*

Melvin had this whole DJ equipment setup in his room; he turned up the music and egged me on to go ahead and dance with his sister. I got up, grabbed her right hand with my left hand and her waist with my right hand and she grabbed my waist with her left hand. We started to dance. Close and very sensual… *it's just how most Spanish dances worked.* All I remember is Joe's sister Maria teaching and telling me to move my feet *(1,2,3 up...1,2,3 up)* and to keep that same motion going the whole song through. It felt so good to be dancing with such a gorgeous girl; but I was imagining I was dancing with Carmella the whole time I was dancing with Melvin's sister, Julinda.

"Oh my God, you dance so good Tyrone!" Julinda excitingly said.

I just smiled at her as I continued to dance and twist her around, acting like I had done it plenty of times before. Melvin was cheering me on as he DJ'd and kept mixing in more songs while Julinda and I danced. I could tell that she was really feeling my skills because she kept smiling at me and getting closer and closer to me while we danced.

After dancing seven straight Bachata songs back to back, we ended the last song almost falling to the floor in joy and laughter.

"Yoooo, Ty! You're really good, my brother; and you know the words to the songs too. That's dope, man!" Melvin exclaimed.
"Thanks, bro. I practice at home all the time. I love Bachata!" I responded.

"That is awesome, I haven't danced like that with a guy in a long time. I loved it! Would you like something to eat and drink?" Julinda asked.

I wanted to say, "Yeah, I'll take something to eat... YOU!!." but I just said, "Yes, please' thank you."

Julinda went into the kitchen and started to prepare food for all of us; but brought Melvin and I two Coronas first. *I know we were only in high school but we were drinking already back then.*

"So, how was your vacation back at home to Jersey City? I remember you briefly telling me about this Dominican girl you liked. What was her name again?" Melvin asked.

"Oh, yea bro. her name is Carmella and I had a great vacation back home." I told him.

"Carmella, that's right! So, what's up bro? Did you get with her? Did you kiss her, did you get her number at least? What's up? Talk to me, my brother?" Melvin eagerly rambled.

"Yoooo, I'm in love with that girl, man! I didn't kiss her yet, not on the lips at least." I laughed. "...but I did get her number though. I was supposed to call her when I got back up here to Trenton; but I haven't yet." I was kicking myself mentally for letting my nerves get the best of me yet again.

"Why haven't you called her yet, bro? You need to call her and keep her interested in you." Melvin told me what I already knew.

"I know, bro. I'm thinking about calling her tonight; but really, I don't know what to say and I don't want to say the wrong things and scare her away from ever talking to me again. You know?" I said, hoping he could relate and give me some good advice.

Melvin nodded. "Yeah, bro. I feel you. Damn, you must really love this girl, yo. Listen, the only advice I can give you is this. You see how you were dancing with my sister and made her smile just by being you? Do the same thing with Carmella, bro. Be you. She'll have no choice but to like you just like my sister did." Melvin said.

"You know what, you are absolutely right, my bro. All I have to do is be myself. I have to go, bro. We will catch up tomorrow, you heard?" I said as I grabbed my things to leave.

"Wait, what about the food my sister is making for you, bro?" Melvin asked.

"Tell her something came up and I had to rush home; but to save it for me. I'll be back again tomorrow." I told him.

"Tato, my brother." Melvin said; which meant "Okay, my brother." in English. He walked me to the door and we peaced each other out.

When I got back outside, the cold hit me right smack in the face. Luckily, I only lived a block away from Melvin. So, I wasn't far from home at all. I needed to leave because I wanted to get my thoughts together for calling Carmella and I wanted to be in the comforts of my own home when I decided to do so. I finally made it home from out of that cold biting ass weather. I swear five minutes felt like thirty.

As I opened the door and walked into my house, I immediately smelled some good food being cooked by my mother in the kitchen. "Hey, Ty!" My mother yelled out to me.

"Hey, mom! How was your day and what is that smelling so good that?!" I asked her as I walked into the kitchen to greet her with a hug and kiss. "I'm cooking some curry chicken and it's going to be excellent! My day was great, thank you for asking. How was your first day back to school?" She asked without looking up from her pan.

"It was good. Everybody had on their new back to school outfits today; but you know your son was the best dressed." I told her.

"That's good, son. Your father wants you to get all the garbage together and put it in front of the house tonight, so the garbage people can pick it up in the morning. Please, don't forget to do that before you go to sleep tonight, thank you." My mother said, totally disregarding my last comment.

"Okay, I won't forget, mom. I'm going upstairs to my room now; but call me when the food is ready, please. Thank you." I said as I was walking away from her, heading upstairs to my room.

I got to my room, opened the door and dropped right onto my bed, looking up at my ceiling fan. All I could think about was what was I going to talk about when I called Carmella; and then it dawned on me. The advice Melvin had just told me at his house and that was to just be myself. I got up off my bed and walked over to my dresser. I pulled open my top drawer and grabbed the piece of paper I had put Carmella number on. I just looked at it for a second; then, I looked at the phone on my other dresser. *I was still a little nervous.* I looked back at the paper again. I did that like five more times before I said to myself, "Let's do this, Ty." I grabbed the phone and my hands started to get a little shaky. I started to dial Carmella number 2~0~1 4~~3~~4~8~9~~6~~~7. The phone started ringing and all I could think to myself was, *what in the world am I doing?*

"Hola?" A woman's voice answered. It was Carmella's mom Angelina.

"Uhmm... yes, hello... Hola Mrs. Angelina, how are you doing? Is Carmella there?" I replied, trying to bury my nerves.

"Ahhh, Carmella ta qui, quien es? (*Ahhh, Carmella is right here, who is this?*) She asked.

"This is Tyrone." I told her.

"Ohhhh, Tyrone!! Como tu estas y donde tu ahora?" (*Ohhh, Tyrone!! How are you and where are you right now?*) She was actually happy it was me calling.

"I'm fine, thank you. I am at home in Trenton now." I responded.

"Oh okay, that's good!! Carmella is right here; hold on and you come back and visit us soon, okay? Tranquilo niño, (Take care son)." She, like most of the Spanish mother's I knew, jumped back and forth between English and Spanish. She yelled out Carmella's name for her to come get the phone.

"Okay, I most definitely will and thank you again." I said back to her.

My heart was beating like the head drummer on a drumline, I was so nervous; but so excited at the same time. I was actually about to speak to the girl of my dreams for the very first time on the phone with no problems.

"Hello?" Carmella's voice came pouring into my ear as smooth as satin.

"Hello, what's up, Mella? It's Tyrone; how you doing?" I replied... remembering to just be myself.

"Tyrone? Oh my God. I'm doing good, how have you been? How was your first day back to school? How's the 11th grade treating you?" She sounded just as happy to hear that it was me calling her.

"My first day back was boring. I was ready to go soon as I got there." I laughed. "But nah, my first day back was pretty cool, no complaints but was ready for the school day to end because I wanted to call you."
"Is that right? Well, I'm glad you did. You made me smile just now. I was actually shocked when my mom told me it was you on the phone. She's

over here being all nosy right now, knowing she only knows a little English." She laughed.

I laughed with her. "That's too funny; but I was just calling to say "hi" and see how you and the fam were doing. You've been on my mind ever since the last time I saw you at your job and I just thought I'd reach out to you, since you did give me your number along with this gorgeous picture of yourself and all." I imagined her blushing and couldn't stop myself from smiling BIG.

"I sure did and I am very happy that you decided to call me, it made my night. I'm about to go take a shower now and get ready for bed. I have to wake up early tomorrow for school; but thank you for calling me again and feel free to call me anytime." She said.

"Okay, love. I'm about to do the same as well but I'll definitely call you again sometime soon. Take my number down off your caller ID and feel free to call me anytime too. I would really love if you did. Other than that, it was good hearing your voice, have a good night and sleep well, Mella." I was giving her my smoothest tone and surprising myself with how relaxed I was coming off.

"Okay, I will do that sooner than you think. Thank you again and you do the same. Talk to you again soon… goodnight, Tyrone." For the first time, I actually heard a hint of nervousness in her voice.

I hung up my phone and fell face flat back on my bed. When I picked myself up, I fell right back onto my bed again about 10 times. I was so happy about how our conversation went that I didn't know what to do with myself. I couldn't believe that I had just called the girl of my dreams and talked with her on the phone. It was only for about five minutes; but it was definitely a start.

I immediately got back on the phone to call Melvin and tell him what had just happened. I had to tell somebody, but he didn't pick up. He must have been asleep already. So, I called my brother Joe to tell him the great news. Boy was he excited for me!

Chapter *7*

High School Basketball Season

About three months had gone by and we were now in the month of December. We had one of the biggest basketball games coming up for my high school against our rival school, Hamilton High West. My JV coach, Coach Allen, told me I would be starting the game because of how well I had been playing in our past games. The Varsity coach had even started to invite me to their practices because I was doing so well on JV. He was ready to move me up and I was hyped and proud of myself about all of this. I was going hard every practice.

The game was finally here and the whole gym was packed with a tremendous amount of people. The JV and Varsity games mattered to everyone who was there to witness the match up. My team stepped onto the court, ready for battle. We knew what the game meant for us, our school and our hometown. We were not leaving that gym without a win.

The referee through the ball up for tip off and my teammate Brian Jefferson who was our center, hit the ball to me. I caught it and the game began. The whole game was a back and forth scoring frenzy between both teams. None of us were letting up or giving the other team any breathing room to take a big lead over each other. Halftime was mostly a rest period and found us all drenched in sweat. Thank God for Gatorade.

Third quarter the score kept close, 45 to 41, their lead. It was the beginning of the fourth quarter and we were down by four points. Coach pulled me to the side and said, "T, now is your time to lead the team home to victory. Now is your time to take over, son. Do what you have to do and bring us home this victory!"

I looked at him and replied, "I got us, coach!"

Walking back onto the basketball court to get ready to start the fourth quarter, I heard a loud familiar voice from the crowd yell out "LET'S GO TY, TAKE OVER, LET'S GO!" I looked up and it was Precious and her friends there cheering me on from the gym bleachers. Even though Precious was now my ex-girlfriend and we were no longer a couple, she still came to my games and supported me because deep down we knew we loved each other. I just had to many other things going on at the time to focus on her. I mean, I practically felt like the man in school. I was getting approached by so many other girls that liked me that it didn't bother me that Precious and I were no longer a couple. Plus, I was still working on securing the main girl I really wanted to be with and that was Carmella. After that first call I made to her back in September, we both kept in touch tremendously. I would call her at least twice every other week and I would take the train back to Jersey City on the weekends when I didn't have basketball practice or I would just miss them if I did. Precious waved at me from the crowd and continued to cheer me on as the buzzer sounded off for the fourth quarter to start. I was very excited and appreciated that she was there. Having that kind of support always made me go harder.

My partner Jarrett was out of bounds when the referee passed him the ball to pass it in bounds to me. Fourth quarter began with a full eight minutes on the clock. For some reason, I felt like Michael Jordan at this very moment in my life. It was a tight net game. Hamilton High was playing press defense on us and we were applying that same pressure on them. I dribbled the ball down the court and got past their press defense. I passed the ball, then got away from the person who was guarding me and went to the baseline corner and waited for the ball to swing back around to me. The ball got back around to me and I was behind the three-point line. I took the shot and all you heard was "SWISH"! I made the shot and the crowd went super wild. We still were down by one point with about six minutes left on the clock; but it didn't matter after that three-pointer went in because my whole team took off after that.

It was like something jumped into all of us after I hit that three-point shot because we all started hitting every shot we took after that. I mean, getting And1's and all. We end up beating Hamilton High West that night by five points. I ended up scoring 27 points, 12 assists, 4 rebounds and five steals. Best game I ever played in High School.

Right after my JV game, the Varsity coach came up to me and said, "Great Job, Tyrone. I want you to come sit on the Varsity bench with the team."

I didn't know what to do with myself. I just said, "Will do; thank you coach!" I had always wanted to be on Varsity and I was finally getting my fair chance be there. After our JV game, Varsity game was up next and I got to sit on the bench with the Varsity team as a player and watched my Varsity team demolish Hamilton Highs Varsity team as well. I was so proud to be a part of that; we celebrated when we got back home and it was such a great time to be alive and witness.

When I finally got to my house, I saw three miss calls from my brother Joe. I said to myself, *this must be important because Joe doesn't ever call back to back like that unless he really needed to talk.* So, I picked up the phone to call him back and to see what was going on. Plus, I wanted to tell him the great news about sitting with the Varsity bench.

"Hello?" Joe answered.

"Yoooo, bro! What's up, man? You won't believe what just happened to me tonight, man! First of all, we won my JV game against our rivals I've been telling you about; but your bro went off! I had 27 points, 12 assists, 4 rebounds and five steals. We Went OFF; but check this out, that's not even the kicker. My damn Varsity coach came up to me after my game and asked me to come sit with the Varsity team and watch the game from the bench, bro! You know that means he wants me on the Varsity team; isn't that great news man!?" I was so excited that everything had just poured out as soon as I heard his voice; but I noticed that he hadn't said anything since I started talking. "Anyway, enough about me. What's up with you, bro? I saw you called three times. You good, man?" I asked.

"First of all, that's really great news, bro! I'm very proud of you; you're doing your thing, man! But I have even better news. You're not going to believe this." Joe said eagerly.

"Better news than what I just told you? Damn, I got to hear this then. What is it, bro? Tell me; tell me, man." I excitingly waited.

"We're going to DR! WE'RE GOING TO DR BRO!! My pops is able to get us $25 buddy passes from his job now because he just got moved up in position at his job in the airport. He said we can fly anywhere we want for $25 now. He said to ask your mom if you could go to DR with us for Christmas break and New year's." Now the words were just pouring out of him.

"Oh snap, yo! I always love going to Dominican Republic with y'all, hell yea!! I'm definitely going to ask her to let me go again; but wait. What am I going to do if the Varsity coach wants me to come practice with them over Christmas break? This might ruin my chances to play Varsity. I don't know, bro. I might be stuck now." I said, already beginning to feel sad. "Listen bro, that's a decision you are going to have to make on your own. I'm just trying to give you an opportunity to see the world as much as possible; but I don't want to take you away from what you got going on over there with basketball. All I'm going to say is… if you do decide to go to DR with us, find out what will happen with your coaches first and then make your decision." Joe said, sounding like he was hiding his disappointment already.

"I hear you, man. Aight, I'm going to have to ask my mom and think this one over because I really do want to go out there, man. Damn. I'll call you back tomorrow when I get home from school, bro. Peace." I said to my brother.

"Okay; no sweat, bro. Hit me up when you get in. Peace." Joe said back and we both ended the call.

I was stuck between a rock and a hard place now. I didn't know what to do because I knew I would have to practice with the team over Christmas break; but I also always wanted to go back to Dominican Republic whenever the opportunity presented itself again. I told my mom that same night and asked her if she would allow me to go with Joe and his family to DR. She happily said "yes". I went back to school that very next morning and immediately all my friends in school were running up to me telling me how great I had played. I was loving the attention; but I didn't even have that game on my mind anymore. I was looking for Coach Allen. I needed to talk to him. I went straight to his office and that's where I found him.

"Tyrone! Just the person I wanted to see! You all played a hell of a game last night, son; and you took over when you needed to. I'm very proud of all of y'all, especially you. In fact, I believe Varsity coach Leonard wants you to start practicing with them after you practice with us, isn't that great!" Coach Allen said, all with the biggest smile I had ever seen on his face.

"Yes, coach. That's awesome news. I'm very happy and excited about this news; but coach I have a question I've been wanting to ask you concerning Christmas break." I said in a serious tone.

"Well, what is it, son?" He asked sensing it must have been important to me.

"Are we going to be practicing around that time because I'm supposed to be going to Dominican Republic with my family and my ticket is booked to go already." I said.

"WHAT?! Are you serious?! Yes, we are going to be practicing every day during that break. The biggest games are coming up after we get back from that break; and if you do decide to go on your trip which is completely fine, you will be benched because that would be unfair to your other teammates who would be coming to practice busting their butts every day. You will also more than likely blow your chances at practicing with Varsity team kiddo. Just being honest with you. You'll definitely have to work your way back up to starting again." Coach Allen said with a look on his face that told me which choice he hoped I'd make correct.

"Wow, I really have to think this over then. Okay, I understand. Thanks, coach. I got to get to first period class, the bell is about to ring." I said, shaking his hand, then sprinting out of his office and down the halls to make it to my first period class on time.

A few weeks went by and Christmas break was near. All I could think about was taking that trip to DR with my bro or staying home for basketball practice to be able to keep my starting position on the team. I was really stuck like some gorilla glue and I had to make a decision very soon. I talked to a few of my close friends at practice who were on the team with me and they all said the same thing, "Go to DR!!." I had made up my mine, there was no way I was going to miss going overseas to another country just to practice basketball. I had weighed out my options and told myself, *it's not like you think you're going to the NBA, so go to DR.*

During practice, I pulled Coach Allen to the side and told him I had to talk to him after practice, in his office. Practice finished and he yelled out, "Tyrone, in my office after you get dressed!" I was pretty shook because Coach Allen was no joke and very hard up with his players, especially his starters. I knew he was going to be let down by my choice; but it's what I chose to do.

"Hey Coach, I had a few weeks to think things over and I've decided to go to DR and experience a new country. This is a once in a lifetime trip for me [I lied because I've been to DR many times before but I had to make it sound good] and I've decided to take the opportunity. I apologize. I know how much this hurts the team; but I've talked to all my other teammates and they told me to go. I really am sorry, coach. I know I probably won't have a starting position anymore when I get back; but I will work very hard to get it back. I just have to go, coach." I said, almost all in one breath.

"Son, I am very disappointed. Not only will you not have a starting position on this team anymore, you will not be on it at all!!" He yelled at me with a slight pause of silence after and then followed with a laugh. "I'm just playing, son!! Hey, I am very happy for you, Tyrone. You should go on that trip. Heck, I would have taken that opportunity too! You go on that trip, have fun, experience life, be safe out there and bring your butt back to practice as soon as you get back because you will have hundreds of suicides to do and a lot of catching up on the new offense/defense I am incorporating, okay?" Coach Allen said with a smile on his face as he patted me on my shoulder.

"Okay, coach. Will do; and thank you for understanding. I will not let you down. Thank you, coach." I said graciously.

"No problem, son. Now, get out of here and don't forget to take a lot of pictures." Coach Allen said back to me as he guided me out of his office.

I left his office with a big smile on my face because I knew I was all the way in the clear to go to Dominican Republic with no problems attached. Life felt so great at this moment.

Chapter 8

DR Trip/Wet Dreams

I knew about how tropical the country called Dominican Republic was, with some of the most beautiful beaches you'll ever see. I knew that it had clear water in the Caribbean with luxury resorts in a town called Punta Cana and some of the most gorgeous women on earth. Well, that's at least what my brother Joe and my friend Melvin had showed me because I thought Melvin's sister and Carmella were two of the most beautiful women in the world and they both were Dominican. At the time, I was heavily infatuated with Latin women. I guess it was because I was always around them growing up with my brother Joe. [Later on in life, I learned to appreciate the beauty and dominance of my black Queens and fell back in love with them. To tell you the truth, I just had a thing for gorgeous women, period. It didn't matter the race but in this particular story, it was a Dominican girl.] I couldn't believe that I was now back on a plane with my best friend and his family going to visit the island for myself once again. This was definitely a dream come true for me because they treated Joe and I like Kings when we were in DR.

When the plane landed in Dominican Republic, everybody on the plane screamed, "YEAHHH" loudly and clapped their hands very abruptly in joy. It made me feel proud to be there. As we were exiting the plane, Joe looked at me extremely excited and said, "We're here, bro! We're HERE!!" He hyped me up even more. I was more than ready to get off the plane. Plus, I was super hungry.

Joe's uncle Jose and his wife Patricia greeted us at baggage claim to help us with our bags and take us to their home after we got all of our bags together. Patricia was one fine woman and I was happy I was going to be staying in her home looking at all of that gorgeousness for two full weeks. She had some very thick legs and wore these tight white booty choker shorts that looked like they were about to burst. She also wore this yellow top that tied around the back of her; it made her breast look so juicy. Being able to see her whole stomach, was a blessing I completely appreciated. Yeah, she definitely was in the gym getting that body right and Jose was definitely working that big voluptuous ass out... if you know what I mean.

We finally arrived at Jose's house, it looked like a humongous mansion to me. It was filled with rooms galore, very spacious and neatly kept. Jose turned on the music and blasted it. I could tell he was very happy to see his family back in DR. Jose went to his fridge, grabbed a whole box of beers called "Presidente", took a beer out for all of us that were there at the house and popped the tops off them all. We all held our beers up to the sky, cheers and started dancing around with each other.

I learned quickly that the rules and laws were very different over in Dominican Republic compared to the United States. If you got into trouble with the law on the streets, you could easily pay the police off right there on the spot and be on your way. So, it was best you keep a lot of money in your pockets, just in case you needed it to get out of a jam. Anyway, as the day continued on, we continued to drink and party. More of Joe's family and friends came over to Jose's house and they all were very happy to see us there. It was like the whole town knew Joe's family. What started as just seven of us quickly turned into 57 of us and this was just the first day of us being there.

The next morning came and it was about 6:30 in the morning and all I heard was roosters crowing very loudly "cock-a-doodle-doo!!" It was the most annoying thing ever, I thought at the time because I was trying to sleep and the roosters were waking me up. I couldn't stand it. "SHUT UPPP!" I yelled out the window at the roosters. I heard laughter coming from the bed Joe was laying on. "What you laughing at over there, them roosters are annoying as fuck. Waking me up out of my sleep. Why do they do that so early in the morning?" I asked Joe.

"Well, the reason for them crowing so early is because back in the day... way before people had an alarm clock to rely on, some people used a rooster to know what time it was in the morning. When that rooster starts crowing, you knew it was about 6ish and it was time to get up and start your day. Even though most people have watches and clocks now, the people here are so used to the roosters crowing in the morning, it has become a part of everyday living for people in this country and that's why they are allowed to crow, bro." Joe explained.

"Ohhhh, I see and get it now. Well, now that you put it that way... I guess it's not all that bad after all." I said.

"Nah, not at all, that was the first history lesson for the day. Now try to get some more sleep, we have a long day ahead of us. Jose is taking us to my parents' house and then we are going to a place called "La Toma" where we get to swim with the fish." Joe said.

"Swim with the fish? What type of place is this? I ain't swimming with no damn fish!" I yelled.

"They're little itty-bitty fish, trust me, bro. You're going to love it and be amazed. Now, go back to sleep and dream of Mella in the meantime." Joe said back to me laughing and at that instance, I put my head back down, put the covers over it and went back to sleep.

About 20 minutes into that sleep, all I could think about was what kind of fish I was going to be swimming with and wishing Carmella was there with me. My eyes were shut and my mind was there at the place called "La Toma" I was dreaming. I envisioned waters flowing down from a mountain rock into a pond full of water and little itty-bitty fish in it swimming around. For some strange reason, there was only one other person at this place; but I was unclear of who she was just yet. I was sitting there on a beach chair enjoying the feel of the sun on my skin and the cool breeze blowing across my body. The water was calling for me to get in it.

The dream got so good that I couldn't even tell you how long I was sleeping for. That's when a pillow hit me upside my head and I heard a voice saying, "Wake up bro, breakfast is ready downstairs." It was Joe; but I couldn't understand how when I was just sitting on a beach chair, trying to see the girl in the water that blurred my vision. I thought it was Carmella, even though I couldn't completely see her.

I was so pissed and confused. "Okay, bro. Getting up now, I'll be downstairs soon. Let me freshen up myself." I told my brother.

"Okay, I'll be downstairs; but try to hurry, man. We have to get ready to go to La Toma today... remember the pool with the fish in it?" Joe said as he left the room to go back downstairs to finish his breakfast.

I was totally confused because I thought I was just at La Toma with Carmella already... the dream had felt so real. As I pulled the covers from over me and propped myself up to sit at the edge of the bed, I noticed that my boxers were a little wet like I had peed on myself or something. I went to the bathroom, closed the door and pulled open my boxers to find I had a little accident in my draws. That's when it all dawned on me, I just had a "Wet Dream" with Carmella in it!

Chapter 9

What Was So Special About April 9?

I had so much fun in DR; it was time well spent there. The island was just as beautiful as the last time I was there. The water was so clear and blue, you could see the fish swimming around and the bottom of the sea. The greenest trees and the most beautiful exotic looking women walking around, everywhere... Every woman we saw looked like God had created her specially as a gift to the world. We partied all night, woke up on the beach, ate until our stomachs were ready to burst, drank beers, hiked in Punta Cana, swam in the bottom of a waterfall with fish, ziplined, and we even road horses. I literally had the time of my life.

My first night there, I had the best dream I've ever had in life this far. I woke up in a small house on the beach and when I stepped outside, Carmella was standing at the water's edge completely naked. I walked up to her and let my hand caress the spine of her back, then traveled my hand lower to cuff her round plumped juicy ass cheeks. "You're so sexy" I whispered in her left ear.

She turned to face me with a seductive smile and said, "Good morning King. Are you hungry? Would you like to eat breakfast?" She kissed my lips between questioning me.

"Yes." I told her. "Go lay my breakfast on the bed." I tapped her on her ass.

She walked away slowly like a kitten into the house and I followed right behind her, enjoying my whole view in front of me. When I got to our bedroom, she was lying there on the bed with her legs spread open, just as I requested for her to do. My breakfast was looking good too. Needless to say, I let my tongue dance all over her body. I woke up from that dream with my lap wet and a smile that lasted all day. I never knew about men having wet dreams but I damn sure loved them.

I felt like the people in DR treated me so well, like a king really. I saw how unfortunate the people were there but how happy they still were; even though they had very little, they were still very happy. I decided to leave both my suitcases full of brand-new clothes and sneakers to Joe's boy cousins and few friends I had met around the neighborhood during this trip back. They were all so very happy and thankful, it made me feel really good inside about what I had done.

After getting back home from vacationing over in Dominican Republic, all I could think about was Carmella. *What was she doing? Was she okay? Should I call her?* The wet dream that I had with her in it was still fresh and in 3D on my brain. I needed to see her soon.

A few more months went by; it was now the beginning of April. April 1st, which was April Fool's day to be exact and basketball season was soon coming to an end with just one more game left before Spring Break. We won our last game of the season and I was thankful it was all over because I could now go to Jersey City more often to see Carmella.

School let out at 2:30 pm and we were officially on Spring Break for two weeks. As soon as I got home, I dropped my bookbag down beside the door and went to grab the cordless phone from out of the kitchen. The phone read "5 missed Calls" and "1 voicemail message" from none other than my bro, Joe. I thought to myself, *Damn, that's a lot of back to back missed calls from him, must be urgent.*

Joe was already in his second year of college, attending this school then called "Jersey City State College"; but it's now known as "New Jersey City University". A school I would also attend after I finished my last year of high school. I hit the voicemail button to play Joe's message.

"YO TY, HIT ME BACK ASAP. YOU GOT TO GET DOWN HERE IF YOU CAN, BRO!! A LOT OF THINGS ARE GOING ON IN THESE NEXT COUPLE OF WEEKS AND TRUST ME, YOU DON'T WANT TO MISS IT! AIGHT, CALL ME BACK, BRO!"

Joe had lots of excitement in his voice. I thought to myself, *I know it's Spring Break and all; but what could be going on that he had to call me five times back to back and leave such an urgent message?* I immediately called Joe back, hoping he was around his phone to answer my call.

"HELLO? TY?!" Joe shouted. I heard loud noises and a lot of people in the background of wherever Joe was.

"Yoo, where the hell you at, bro? It's loud as fuck in there. I can't really hear you!" I responded.

"HOLD ON, HOLD ON! I CAN'T HEAR YOU THAT GOOD! LET ME GET OUT THIS SPOT SO I CAN HEAR YOU BETTER! HOLD ON!" Joe shouted back at me as it sounded like he was walking away from the noisy place he was in. "Yo, can you hear me now, good. It's a day party going on over here at the college. They're having them all week to try to recruit and sign new people up to attend the college. I was calling you to tell you that you should come down here and sign up being that it's your last year of high school next year. That way, you'll already be ahead of the game when it comes to doing that. Plus, we could chill on campus and you would get to get a feel for the college life early. You'll already know about it by the time you get here. Oh yeah, I forgot to tell you... Carmella family is throwing a surprise birthday party for her in 1 week from now. Her birthday is April 9th but that day lands on a Sunday. So, they're going to throw it on Saturday, the day before, on the 8th to catch her off guard and surprise her. YOU HAVE TO GET DOWN HERE, MAN!" Joe shouted intensely, sounding like he had the biggest smirk on his face.

"Oh, for real!? That's what's up; because I'm officially on Spring Break for two and a half weeks starting today. I'm on the next train down there! I'll see you soon, bro!" I said back to Joe as we both said "OK" to one another and hung up the phone.

I grabbed my book bag from the door, ran upstairs to my room, took my big suitcase out of my closet and packed like I was going away for a year. I took a taxi to the Trenton train station to catch the 5:15 pm New Jersey Transit Train to Newark Penn Station. This was the train I took mostly every other weekend back to Jersey City all of the five years I had been living in Trenton.

I finally made it to Joe's house, exhausted as ever from moving around with that big ass suitcase. Joe burst into laughter soon as he opened his house door and saw me.

"What the hell are you laughing at, man? Move, I need some damn water!" I said to Joe as he laughed at me even harder. He laughed so hard that he fell to the ground. "Yooo! You got here quick as hell! I just spoke to you… and what the fuck did you pack, for both of us!?" Joe laughed harder and harder, crying tears of humor at this point.

"Shut up, man!" I said to Joe, laughing as well.

"No; but the real joke is… I was just April Fooling you about everything! Ahhhhh!!" Joe said, laughing hard as fuck at me with tears coming out of his eyes.

"WHAT!! ARE YOU SERIOUS RIGHT NOW!!! YOU CAN'T BE FUCKING SERIOUS!! ARE YOU JOKING OR FOR REAL, BRO; BECAUSE I KNOW IT'S APRIL FOOL'S DAY AND ALL BUT IF

YOU ARE SERIOUS RIGHT NOW ABOUT GETTING ME LIKE THIS WE'RE ABOUT TO FIGHT, REAL TALK!" I said to my brother, already starting to get angry. Before he could even answer, I was rushing him and wrestling him on the floor.

"Nah! Nah, chill bro, I'm just joking. I'M JUST JOKING!! EVERYTHING IS REAL, WHAT I SAID ON THE PHONE WAS ALL FOR REAL!! GOT YOU TWICE IN ONE DAY!! AHHHH!!" Joe said, laughing again.

At this point, I didn't know if he was playing or not; but all I knew was that I didn't care anymore because it was always fun to be back home and I knew staying there for two weeks, I would eventually get to see Carmella sometime anyway.

For the next few days, Joe and I would attend the festivities going on at the college. Although it was just the summer of 1999 and I still had one more year left of high school, I signed up and put in my application to attend the college come September of 2000. Being there and being a part of what the college had going on really was a great experience for me to get a real good feel for college life. I got to roam around all over the campus, I ate for free and the cafeteria food was BANGING! I got to play basketball with some of the college players that were on the team already which was great because I planned on trying out for the team. Joe and I were like the reigning champions in the game room when it came to ping pong tournaments. I met a few fine girls that attended the school and some that were going to be attending the college in the future. We went to some parties they were throwing… that was the bomb. I was living life, in a complete fantasy real world, and I was loving it.

A few days of partying went by and Joe and I were still ready for more to come. We would drive around the city in the Lexus or the Benz, blasting the music we loved or blasting the hip hop music I recorded at the studio. I always had dreams of being this big rap star, ever since my mom and dad took me to see Big Daddy Kane perform in concert at the

Apollo in Harlem New York when I was like 7-years-old. It was the greatest experience of my life to see how Kane moved and soothed the crowd. I'll never forget it. Everybody in the audience was standing up and I couldn't really see at first but then my dad put me on his shoulders and then I had the clearest view. When the curtains opened up, all you saw was a bubble bath on stage with Big Daddy Kane in it smoking on a huge cigar. As I got older and watched a few gangster movies, I knew where he got the idea to do that from, the movie "Scarface". There was a similar scene in that movie that was very popular, where the actor "Al Pacino" is in a bubble bath smoking on a cigar. In those days rappers was very infatuated with the mob movies and gangster lifestyle; so, they tried to emulate them. Anyway, Big Daddy Kane is in a bubble bath with a cigar in his mouth and all you heard come out of the DJs speakers was "(beat) I'm going to give it to yuh...(beat)(beat)...I'm going to give it to yuh, give to yuh, give it to yuh (Big Daddy Kane's Lyrics) "Well, excuse me, take a few minutes to mellow out, Big Daddy Kane's on the mic and I'm going to tell about.." As soon as he started rapping, the whole crowd went wild and started screaming; especially the ladies, as he rapped his lyrics. Getting up and stepping out of the bath tub with only boxers on and nothing else, he had women going crazy over him. I mean, I saw women throwing their panties on stage and I knew right then that I wanted to be a rapper.

It was Friday; and Joe and I decided we wanted to go shoot some hoops at Lincoln park and try to get a full court game going. So, we rode over to the park. On our way there, we started a conversation about Carmella's surprise birthday party her family was having for her tomorrow. Joe turned down the music. "Yo Ty, you know Mella' surprise birthday party is tomorrow at 7pm, right? Did you get her a gift yet? If not, what are you going to get her? Whatever it is, it has to be different from anything she is used to getting. Oh yea, I been wanting to tell you something too, bro. I just didn't want to make you feel all bad... but I got to tell you, man. I think Mella got a new boyfriend, man!" Joe said in a sad tone.

"Yeah? Damn, man. Who is he? Do you know for sure, bro? And I got some ideas of what I want to get her but I'm not completely sure yet man. I don't even know what she really likes." I admitted.

"I don't know either; but after we go play ball, we could go over her house and find out. Sariah is supposed to be going over there later too. I could act like I want to go see her while she's over there and bring you with me. Then, we could try to find out what's some of the things she really likes." He got quiet for a few seconds. "Yea man; but I'm pretty sure she has a new boyfriend. I met him once while I was there, his name is Len or Lenny or something like that… but forget about him, he ain't got nothing on my brother. I heard through the grapevine that he don't be treating her right at all. So, you still got a chance; and anyway, that's your wife so forget about him." Joe said with a grin of confidence on his face. I just know I heard her mention that name Lenny to me before some years ago, I thought to myself. She must be back with him.

"Yeah, you right. Forget about him; that's my wife! I don't care who he is, he better start treating her right before I slip in and snatch her away from his stupid ass." I said with a smirk on my face; but inside I was disappointed and sad that Carmella had a new man. "Anyway, let's go over to her house after we go play ball; I definitely want to see her and try to figure this damn gift out. I got to make her remember me with what I get her for her birthday." I said to Joe with the most serious face on.

After winning like seven in a row, full court games, we were tired and ready to stop playing ball for the day. As Joe and I grabbed our bags from off the bench in the park, we started to walk back towards the car, cracking jokes about how we were doing everybody dirty on the court. Then Joe's phone rang.

"Hello?" Joe picked up and answered. "Yeah, they cooked? We hungry like a mug. Word! Okay, babe. Me and Ty on our way!" Joe ended his call and turned to me. "Yooo, that was Sariah; and she said Mella' mom,

Angelina, cooked some real good food. We're about to go over there right now. You hungry, right?" Joe had the biggest smile on his face.

"Absolutely!! Let's go!!" I said, very excited that we were about to go to Carmella's house. We got in the car and drove off, headed to downtown Jersey City. We pulled up in front of this five-story apartment building, got out the car and proceeded through the entrance doors of the apartment building and headed towards a flight of steps. Carmella lived on the third floor and the closer we got to her floor, the more you smelled the food her mother was cooking. When we finally got to their apartment, the door was slightly cracked already. I guess to let out the heat from the food Angelina was cooking and the food was smelling oh so good. Joe still rung the little bell that was on the door and knocked rapidly before pushing the door open and walking right in like he had been there plenty times before already. I followed his lead and walked right in as well.

As soon as you walk into their apartment, you see the kitchen right in front of you and Angelina standing in it cooking up a feast. "Oh Yea!! Joe? Tyrone? Come in, come in!" Angelina said, greeting us both at the door with hugs and kisses on the cheek. Sariah came out the bathroom to the kitchen area to greet us as well and took us to the living room where everyone else was. As we are walking towards the living room, I see Carmella walk into a bedroom in the back of the apartment and all I could think to myself was, *Yes, she is here!* I did wonder why she looked like she was mad. Then, as we got into the living room, who else did I see sitting there on the couch looking like a scrub? The bum Joe pointed out to be her new boyfriend, Lenny. I thought to myself, He must have pissed her off. I kept my composure and shook his hand; but I was heated he was there though because I didn't know how I was going to be able to really talk to Mella. I got lucky and he got up not too long after we sat down and stormed out of the apartment, saying no goodbyes to anyone. I thought to myself again, *Yes! Get the fuck out of here conyaso* (shithead) *and don't ever come back either!*

Sariah served Joe and I some food and put a good movie on. Carmella mom Angelina joined us in the living room and sat right next to me, trying to talk to me in English but she wasn't that good at it yet. She was very interested in me and was very nice to me as well. All I could think of was not seeing Carmella ever since I got there. She hadn't come out of that room since she went in it. I knew that guy Lenny must have really pissed her off. So, I asked Sariah, "Where is Carmella? Is she okay? Tell her to come out and watch the movie with us. Tell her, I came to see her."

Sariah got up, went to the room Carmella was in, I'm guessing she told her what I said because Sariah came back out and said to me, "She said okay Ty, she'll be out in a sec."

I was super happy Sariah came back out and said that because I hadn't seen Carmella in months; we just talked on the phone a few times, ever since the time I got back to Trenton and that was it. Carmella walked out the room she was in, looking like a sweet honeycomb beehive to a hungry brown bear. She had these tight jeans on that brought out every God giving curve on her voluptuous ass and thighs. She had this red shirt on, with the cartoon character "Winnie The Pooh" pouring a jar of honey in his mouth on it, right where Carmella beautiful breast laid. I started to think to myself, *Oh how I wish I was Winnie The Pooh right now.* She greeted Joe and I with a kiss on the cheek and sat down on the couch right next to me as her mom got up and went into that same room Carmella had just came out of.

"So, what are you guys watching?" Carmella whispered softly into my ear.

"Bad Boys, with Martin Lawrence and Will Smith in it. It's pretty dope too." I whispered back to her, taking a quick glance at her now that she was up close and personal with me sitting next to her. She caught me staring at her; but she just smiled and got really comfortable in the couch beside me. She even rested a piece of her back on my chest. I was so nervous inside at this point. I couldn't believe I was really chilling with the girl of my dreams, on her couch with her relaxing herself on my chest and on her birthday week at that... but I was. The movie was just about finished and it was about 11:45 at night. Carmella practically fell asleep on my chest... in my arms. She looked so peaceful, sleeping on me, I didn't want to wake her; but Joe was ready to go. So, I had to.

Sariah and Joe got up. "Come on, bro. Wake sleeping beauty up; it's time for us to get out of here. We have to get up early tomorrow. I'll be waiting out in the hall for you with Sariah. Don't forget to give her that." Joe said to me, nodding his head in the direction of the gift I put down under the kitchen table when I first walked in the apartment. I almost completely forgot about it, watching the movie but I was happy as ever he reminded me about it. Joe and Sariah walked out of the apartment.

"Mella, Mella. Mella, come on wake-up, love. We are about to leave, wake up." I said to Carmella, tapping her on the outside of her thigh. She woke up slowly and said, "Okay, Ty; thanks for coming to spend time with me. I really enjoyed this." As we both got up, hugged and kissed each other on the cheek, we started to walk towards the kitchen. Before going to Carmella house, Joe and I went back to our house and sat downstairs in our basement, thought long and hard about what makes Carmella happy. We had called Sariah earlier in the week to find out some things she knew about her cousin. All we got out of her was that she is really infatuated with the cartoon character "Winnie The Pooh". So, Joe and I went to the mall and I bought a few items out of the Disney store after we got dress and left our house, right before stopping over Carmella house. I got a bunch of "Winnie The Pooh" items. Along with that, I wrote her a Birthday song and rapped it for her on a cassette tape. I also wrote her a love letter detailing how much I adored her. She also got a rose from me and chocolate along with a whole outfit for herself to wear. These were all the items I had in a big birthday bag I had under her kitchen table for her. Before we got to her door, I stopped her and said, "Hold on, I almost forgot." I squatted down and grabbed the gift bag and the rose from under the table. I smiled wide as I gave it to her. "Happy Birthday, my love. I hope you really like what I got for you. I put a lot of thought into it and wanted to be the first to give you an early birthday present. Please don't look at it until I leave." I said to Carmella as she looked at me like she was about to cry.

"Awww, thank you sooo much, Ty! This is so nice of you; I did not even expect this from you. You just touched my whole entire heart, thank you again so much!" She said, hugging me tightly. "Hahaaa, anytime love, I really like you, Mella. So, make sure you read what I wrote to you and listen to the music in there as well. Call me sometime tomorrow and I'll try to stop by again tomorrow too. Happy Birthday again; and have a good night, love." I said back to Mella as we gently let each other go from the tight embrace we were still lock in on.

She said, "Okay; I will and thank you again."

She looked up into my eyes and I knew my chance when I saw it. She pressed her breast against my chest softly and I wrapped my arms back around her waist and it happened. We leaned in and kissed each other. Just on the lips at first, then she slowly parted her lips to let my tongue slip between them. In that moment, it felt like she was giving herself to me. Like the universe was confirming that she would eventually be mine. Her body relaxed a little in my arms, it was like she melted onto me. I can't say how long the kiss lasted because, time really felt like it stopped. Yeah, it was definitely a love story in the making. One I felt someday I'd probably write about. This girl really was the love of my life.

We stopped kissing and I stepped out of her house to find Joe and Sariah sitting on the stairwell, waiting for us to come out. We all had big smiles on our faces like we all knew what just happened.

"Ready, bro? Let's go, it's late as hell!" I said to Joe as he got up, hugged Sariah and gave her a kiss. As we were about to go down the steps, I took one look back at Carmella, who was still at her door and I said "Don't forget to call me."

She smiled at me and said, "I got you; I won't forget."

Joe and I continued down the stairs, exited the building and got in our car. After a knowing glance at one another, we took off, riding back to our house. "So, what happened? What happened when you gave her the gift, man? What happened!?" Joe anxiously asked me.

"Nothing happened...she said why did you get me this. I don't want it, please get out of my house." I lied.

Joe knew I was bullshitting from the little smirk I couldn't keep off my face. "Yeah right, she didn't say that. Come on, man. Tell me what happened!!" Joe said, eager to know what happened in that house.

"Okay; I gave her the gift and rose, told her I really liked her and wanted her to read the letter and listen to the music very carefully. That there were deep messages from me, in there for her to know how I really felt about her. She was so excited and surprised that I even got her a gift and knew it was her birthday, she just thanked me and hugged me tightly. Right after she let me go, we leaned in to say goodbye to each other with a normal kiss on the cheek. Bro, then she looked up at me and it just happened. Carmella and I kissed!! We tongued each other down!!" I told Joe.

"WHAT!! YOU KISSED EACH OTHER!! MY BROTHER!! YOU ARE IN THERE, MAN!! THAT'S IT, YOU GOT HER! SHE'S GOING TO BE YOUR WIFE!!" Joe screamed at me.

"I don't know, man. I'm praying for that to become the truth. I told her not to look at anything until we left her home and to call me tomorrow. So, we'll see what happens; but yea I know I'm definitely getting closer to her heart, bro. I'm super proud of myself right now; real talk." I told my brother as we continued to talk about the same thing over and over again on the ride back home to our house. The next night Joe and I showed back up to Angelina's house to help the rest of the family surprise Mella for her birthday. It was a wonderful celebration and I always looked forward to April 9th coming around every year. It was a very special day to me.

Chapter *10*

10 Our Birthday Party (July)

It was June 19, pretty much the last week of my 11th grade year in high school. It had been about two months since I last saw Mella on her birthday in April. We had spoke on the phone about three times in that two-month time period because Joe would always be going over Carmella house with his girlfriend Sariah to hang out with her family and he would always put her on the phone so that I could say hello. Carmella and I would always share a laugh or two every time we spoke. She would always tell me how much she liked my gift that I put together for her on her birthday and I would always tell her that I couldn't wait to see her when I come to spend the whole summer in Jersey City. I would also joke with her about how she couldn't dance bachata better than me.

Bachata was Dominican music I learned how to dance with Joe and his parents. I loved to dance to Bachata because you got to hold the girl you were dancing with very close to you and really feel the love you had for one another as you both danced and moved your legs and hips. [1-2-3 leg up, 1-2-3 leg up.] That's how you dance bachata, it was that simple to learn and I got really nice at dancing it. Carmella would tell me over the phone, that I better know how to dance by time I got down to Jersey City for the summer because she was going to run me off the dancefloor. I loved the sound of that every time she said it to me. All I could think about was having both her arms around my neck, as I guided her waist in the direction I wanted it to go, with us looking each other in the eyes dancing to one of Raulin Rodriguez's songs.

School had finally let out and everybody said their last goodbyes until next year. I went straight home after school. I had my bags packed from the night before; and I was ready to be in Jersey City already. My parents were still at work by the time I came home but they knew my plans already. I caught the bus to the Trenton train station, purchased a New Jersey Transit ticket, gave the conductor my ticket and got on the train with my bags. I was so excited to be going back to Jersey City.

Joe met me at the Newark Penn Station. He was driving a brand-new silver Mercedes Benz; I was hyped. I got in the car and the first thing he said to me was, "Yo, I think Mella really likes you, bro. I don't know but every time I go over there, she always bringing your name up. We have to figure out a major game plan for y'all to chill a whole lot this summer so that you can wife that up, man. For real."

I was looking at Joe with the biggest smile on my face. "I knowww, she keeps telling me she is going to scrub me on the dance floor when we dance bachata." I chuckled. "We have to take them out dancing or set up a party of some sort. Speaking of parties, what are we doing for our birthday, bro? We should throw ourselves a party?"

Joe looked at me with a look on his face like a seven- year- old kid that had just gotten taken to the chocolate factory or candy shop. "Yoooo, that's a great idea. We can invite all of Sariah cousin's and some of my sister's friends, bring some of our boys and throw a huge party! Ok, we only have about a week and a half to put this thing together and make it come alive. So, soon as we get to the house, let's start planning everything out."

I was definitely with everything he had just said to me and we did just that. We got on the phone for the next few days and started inviting everyone to our party. We even solidified the spot where we were going to throw it, our friend Los' house. Days were getting shorter and the party was getting closer. Joe and I decided to throw our party on the 7th of July, which was a Saturday and landed in between both our birthdays.

The day of the party, it didn't take long for Los' house to get Jam packed. I mean, the ladies and the fellas were coming in from all over the place. I even think some of the college students that lived on Los' block had even tried to get into the party.

An hour later, Sariah and her cousins finally pulled up to the party and parked their car. Sariah brought all her cousins with her. I even saw Carmella walking with them down the block from where they parked.

"Ohhh snap! Yo, Ty! That's Mella and all her sisters, bro; she came dog! Yo, this party is about to be off the chain!" Joe said excitingly to me and the rest of the fellas that were hanging in the front entrance of the house.

"Yeah, I see her sexy ass. Welp fellas, ONCE AGAIN IT'S ON!!" I said to my boys as Sariah, Carmella and the rest of her sisters approached us at the door.

"$30!!" Joe said to Sariah who led the pack of six.

"WHAT?" Sariah said back with a frown on her face.

"$30, it's six of you. So, that'll be $5 each head... $30!!" Joe explained with a serious look on his face.

"Paaaaa!! Move, Joe! Don't try to make us pay because yo boy Tyrone can't see me in Bachata!" Carmella said, shoving Joe to the side looking me dead in my face with the cutest smirk. Then she walked into the party with the rest of her squad.

"OHHHHHH!" Everybody chanted out as all of us guys followed all of Carmella and Sariah's squad into the party.

Carmella was looking gorgeous as ever. She wore this one-piece leather tight outfit that practically showed every curve on her body. She literally and physically looked like "Catwoman" in the flesh. I swear this felt like a Kid and Play scene from the movie House Party though. The party was jamming soon as we all walked in and I remembered it clear as day what song had come on. It was this song titled "Vagabundo, Borracho y Loco" by a guy named "Kiko Rodriguez" and I loved this song. It was fast paced but had a very smooth groove to it. After popping lip about me outside, Carmella decided she wanted to try and sit down on the empty couch when we got inside.

"Ohhh, No, No, Nooo sweetheart, don't try to sit down now. It's time for me to teach you a little lesson, my love." I said to her as I grabbed her hand and guided her to the dancefloor. Carmella looked at me with a gentle smile on her face, as if she couldn't wait to dance with me. I felt the same way. As we proceeded to walk to the middle of the dancefloor in the living room, it's like everybody on the dancefloor made a big circle around us and cheered us on as we started to dance with each other. *1,2,3 leg up, 1,2,3 leg up...*

Carmella and I were doing some real sensual moves on each other. I swear dancing with her, I felt like nobody was around us. Like it was just her and I in the room. The way she was looking into my eyes as we danced, had me thinking all kinds of thoughts in my head. At that instance, I closed my eyes just for a moment and I imagined my life with Carmella and it was so great. We were married with children like the old TV show with Al and Peggy Bundy and their children, lol. Nah but seriously, we really loved each other and showed it every single day. The swaying motion of our bodies moving in rhythm together just always felt like our bond was so close.

Then the bachata song that was playing ended and all I heard was... "Now, who's hot, who's not...Tell me who rock, who sell out in the stores...You tell me who flopped, who copped the blue drop... Who jewels got rocks... who's mostly Dolce down to the tube sock... the same old pimp Mase, you know ain't nothing change but my limp." It was a "The Notorious B.I.G. ft P.Diddy and Mase" song titled "Mo money, Mo problems" It instantly snapped me out of my imagination land.

Everybody in the party rushed back to the middle of the dancefloor when that song came on and started dancing and singing the song word for word. It was the most popular song at the time. Mella and I continued to dance to it as well; jumping up and saying the words. All her sisters and all my boys all joined in. We were having so much fun that night, I wish it had never ended.

As everyone continued to party the night away, I grabbed Carmella's by her hand and told her to follow me. I knew she had to be thirsty at this point after all that dancing; we all were sweating. We had the four fans circulating in the party but it still was super-hot in there with all the people that were there. Anyway, I walked Mella to the kitchen area and fixed both of us a plate to eat and got us both cold drinks with ice in the cups. I told her to follow me to the backyard where we could get some fresh air, sit and eat our food. She followed me, I felt she trusted me so much at this point. So, I treated her like she was my wife already. I pulled the zipper up on the tent, where the boys and I would go to talk about serious situations, in the backyard of Los house (*you remember*). We walked inside of the tent and sat down on the extended bench chair that was in there.

"Thank you for fixing me a plate and getting me something to drink, Ty. I was starting to get drained in that hot ass place." She giggled. "So, where did you learn how to dance Bachata like that? You are wayyy better than I thought you would be. I mean, you aight, punk." She giggled again before biting into her chicken wing.

"Yeah, I know you felt me on that dancefloor. I shocked that ass, didn't I?" I laughed. 'Nah; but for real, I learned how to dance Bachata when I recently went to DR with Joe's family but I been in love with the music. You not too bad yourself, punk." I laughed again. "So, how have you been otherwise? How's your mom, job, that guy that went storming out your house that day I came over for your birthday?" This time, we both laughed.

"My mom is doing okay. She is still very much upset and sad though on how my father was done in that whole court situation. The job is cool, I just be working, working, working. I'm really trying to save up so that I can get my own place in the future. You see how many people live in my mother's house, six of us that lives in that little ass apartment. Plus, my twin sisters' boyfriends be there all day too. So, eight of us." We both shook our heads then giggled when we notice how in sync we were. "All jokes to the side though, I love my fam and all; but I never get any privacy over there. So, as soon as I save up enough money to get my own place, I'm out. As far as the asshole that stormed out of my house that day you and Joe came over, that's my soon-to-be ex-boyfriend. He gets on my last nerve; he doesn't really appreciate me. He doesn't make me feel wanted. You know, that day of my birthday, you see how you put all that stuff together for me… I could tell you put some thoughts, feeling and love into that and it touched my heart because I love stuff like that. It makes me feel good as a woman and wanted but him, No. He bought me a pair of sneakers, dropped it off and said "happy birthday". A couple hours went by and we were just sitting there. When you and Joe came, he got up and left. Like who does that? Before y'all came there, he wasn't showing me any special attention at all anyway. So, I didn't really care that he left and I was really happy to see you too." Carmella confessed, as it was starting to feel like a scene from the movie "Coming to America" where Eddie Murphy (I mean Akeem) went to go cater to Lisa McDowell after being embarrassed by her boyfriend Darrell at the time. Darrell announced an engagement to Lisa without her knowing or hearing anything about it, right in front of his and her friends and family and she was not having it. So, she stormed out the house, brought him to the garage, told him off and basically dumped him. Then after doing that, Lisa went into her dad's backyard to sit on the swing that was back there and Akeem went to comfort her with a beverage and sat next to her on another swing and small talked with her, making her smile. They basically fell in love from that point on. That's exactly what I wanted to happen for Carmella and I. I wanted to tell her to dump Lenny, let me be her man and she would always forever feel wanted by me... but I just said, "Damn, dude must be a fool not to make you feel wanted. You're everything a man could ever wish for from a woman. When you become my girl, I'm going to treat you like the queen you are and you'll be always happy with wanting me around. What an idiot he is."

"Yes, he is a big idiot. I can't stand him!" She said back to me and suddenly she turned more toward me, grabbed my hands and said. "Thank you again, Ty. I'm really glad I came out to this party; I'm having so much fun. I don't even have fun anymore because that asshole doesn't even take me anywhere. All I do is go to school, go to work and sit in my room at home. Boring ass life I live; but I said to myself, let me get out and go see what this party is about. I'm so happy I did!" She said to me, embracing me with a long, tight hug.

As she let me go, I heard some voices start to get close, coming towards where we were sitting in the tent. I looked Mella in her eyes, and she looked me in mine. I gently grabbed her face with both of my hands and said to her, "Mella, thank you for coming to my party. You don't know how much you made my night... but you really did. I'm on cloud nine with you right now; and I thank you, love." Then, it happened again. We kissed each other. This time, we were really tongue wrestling. The voices got louder and closer, so we stopped. I kissed her on her forehead and she smiled at me.

Then we heard, "Ah ha! Here you two lovebirds are, everybody's been looking for you two. We all want to see y'all dance Bachata again in the battle we are about to have. Come on!!" It was Joe and Sariah; they both came out to get us to take Mella and I back inside to dance.

They put on this song titled, "Quiero Saber De Ti" by a guy named "Bienvenido Rodriguez" followed up by another song from a band called "Los Toros Band" and the song title was, "Quizas Si, Quizas No". It was the perfect song to end the night dancing with Mella because even though I didn't understand much of what they were saying in the song at that time, it sounded like the guy was passionately telling the girl in that song to forget those other guys she had been dealing with. It sounded like he was telling the girl that she was the one for him and he was the one for her and that's exactly how I felt and what I wanted Carmella to know from me. As the song was ending, Mella and I were hugged up close dancing and the party was pretty much over. Everyone was getting their stuff and heading out of the door.

"Hey, hold on Mella. I want to walk you out to y'all car." I said to her.

"Okay, cool. Come on; I think Joe and Sariah are up there already." She said back to me, as we started to head up the block towards where Sariah had parked her car.

"So, you work tomorrow? What time do you get off? I might stop by to say hi." I asked as we held each other's hand and walked.

"Unfortunately, yes I do work tomorrow. I go in at 1pm and get off around 9:30 pm. You should come and see me though; I would love that." She said as we finally approached Sariah's car.

"Bet, I'll definitely come see you tomorrow and the next day too if you work again and want me to." She giggled and we gave each other a really long, tight hug and kiss on the cheeks. We didn't want everyone all in our business just yet, so we kept it cool in front of others for the most part but tonight was different and we both definitely knew what it was and so did everyone else. I opened her door and all you heard was her sisters in the back saying, "Mella, come on. Kiss him already." As they all giggled.

She leaned in and pressed her soft lips up against mine. She parted her lips for me again and I was on my way to cloud nine when we heard… "OOOOH!" She snatched away, embarrassed. I kissed her lips innocently again in a quick peck.

"Thank you, Joeee! Thank you, Tyyyy, we had a great time!! Come on, Mella!" Sariah said after kissing her man.

Carmella got into the car and I shut her door for her. Joe yelled out for Sariah to buckle up, drive safe and call him when they got home. Sariah beeped the horn and drove off.

"YOOOOO! That girl is in love with you Tyyyy! Hahaaa! You did it, man! She likes you heavy now bro; I could tell!! She was really, really, really feeling how you danced with her, bro!! You got to go to her job like every other day now, man. Just keep popping up and surprising her so you stay on her mind." Joe said excitingly.

"Oh, fo sho! That's what I plan to do, bro." I nodded, feeling satisfied with myself. "Yeah, we really bonded heavy tonight. I'm up at her job asap tomorrow, bro and if she needs a ride home... we going to make that happen for her too." I said back to Joe as we entered back into Los' house mad excited.

Chapter *11*

The Feeling's Mutual (Confessions)

A couple of years went by since that amazing Saturday night party we had at my friend Los' house. Since then, I graduated high school and just finished my first semester at New Jersey City University. Carmella was about to finish her last year of high school. After I graduated from high school, I moved back to Jersey City so that I could be closer to Carmella and attend college. In between the years that just gone by, Mella and I became even more close. Being that Joe remained dating Carmella's cousin Sariah still, whenever Carmella and Sariah's family threw parties or had events, we would always be invited to join them. You can say we were all like family.

Around this time, I had my license so I was driving my own wheels. Well… not necessarily my own wheels, my aunt Delores would always let me borrow her Range Rover truck whenever I asked to use it, and that would be frequently. I got so close with Carmella and her family that I would just pop up at their house with a box of Coronas in my hands and just spend the whole day with them. I could pop up any day of the week, at any time and I was never turned away. I usually went to their house on the weekends and early in the daytime. I felt those were the more appropriate days and times to visit them. Whenever I went over to her house, her mother would be so excited to see me. Sometimes Carmella wouldn't even be there because she was at work and I would stop by and her mother would still allow me to come in and spend the day with her. She would give me some money and say "Tyrone, go buy some Coronas for us" and continued cooking her food. That is another reason why I loved going over Carmella house, her mother's food was so deliciously addictive. I mean, I would sit there for hours with her, drinking Coronas, watching her cook, talking to her, all while listening to the bachata music that was playing from the living room. She had a really nice sound system.

Another reason why I would be over Carmella house so much is because her and her boyfriend Lenny's relationship was not doing too well at all. Carmella would stress this to me every time I went to pick her up from work when Lenny was supposed to pick her up and he didn't. She was really getting fed up with him and his ways towards her. Carmella's job was at least an hour's walk away from where she lived and this dude Lenny would not pick up his phone nor show up to her job when it was time for her to get off of work. Luckily, she gave me note of this, one late night I stopped by her job to visit her while she was just getting off of work and it was about to rain drastically. She was standing in front of her supermarket when I pulled up to her in the parking lot and rolled down my passenger window. "Hey gorgeous...What's a pretty woman like you doing standing out here all alone? Where's your bodyguard that's supposed to be holding your umbrella?" I said jokingly to Carmella with a smirk on my face.

"OH MY GOD, TY!! I'M SO HAPPY TO SEE YOU HERE!! IT'S ABOUT TO POUR DOWN OUT HERE; CAN I GET IN?" Carmella asked in the sweetest tone.

"YOU STILL OUT THERE? GET IN!!" I yelled back at her... I reached over and opened the passenger door for her and she quickly hopped into my truck as the rain started to pour down. She shut her door, turned back around, gave me a hug and three kisses on my right cheek saying, "Thank you! Thank you! Thank you so much for being here, Ty. You are always on time. I don't know where this Asshole is (referring to her boyfriend Lenny), probably out with some skank! I'm so tired and irritated with him, ughhh! But that's ok though because our days together are numbered; it's a wrap for this relationship, I swear!" Carmella said with a very frustrated and angry voice as I drove off to park the truck and wait with her for her ride. Those words she uttered to me were good music to my ears though.

"I feel you, love; and it's raining too. What time was he supposed to be here?" I asked Carmella with a sincere concerned facial expression.

"Raining is not the word, look at it out here. It's POURING! It looks like a damn storm out here. I got off at 9:45pm, I told that idiot to be here at 9:30pm and wait 15 minutes until I got off at 9:45pm. Soon as I get off, he usually picks me up from the same spot you picked me up from just now. I called his phone five times now; no answer! And it's not like I can think maybe something happened to him because I have before but this is a constant thing he does to me all the time. Then, I either have to take the bus home or even worse…walk!" Carmella said to me angrily.

I couldn't stand to see her ever upset, mad, or angry. It really bothered my soul. "Don't worry about it, I'll tell you what… Give me a call anytime you feel you need to be picked up and I'll try my best to make it to you or at least get you home safely, I don't care if I have to call a taxi for you, I'll do it. In the meantime, we will just wait here for him to show up because he is supposed to be picking you up, right? Maybe he got stuck in traffic or something. I don't know; but I have no problem waiting here with you until he comes and if he doesn't show up within the next 20/30 minutes, I'll take you home. Okay, my love?" I said to her.

"Okay, thank you so much Ty. I really appreciate having you in my life and the things you've done for me through the years of knowing each other. It really means a lot to me." She said back to me, putting her hand on top of mine as I rested it on the middle console.

We sat there in the truck with the music playing low in the parking lot for about 35 minutes to an hour. We got so into our conversation; we didn't even realize how fast time was pasting by. We talked about everything, from her really being done with high school, how she couldn't wait to graduate in two weeks and be done with it all, to her wanting to move out of her mother's apartment and getting her own place. She didn't really know what she wanted to do after she graduated high school but she did want to finish. I mentioned getting her registered for college. I told her it would be easy to get her in because my sister Tammy was one of the people who worked at the University admissions office and all I would have to do was give my sister Carmella name. She was very excited and very interested about hearing those details. We also talked about her not wanting to be with Lenny anymore. She was completely over him; especially after tonight with him not showing up on time and me having to sit there and wait with her. She also confessed her love for me that night and I finally confessed mine; but that wasn't until we drove off and got in front of her apartment building. See, what happened was, Lenny finally showed up to her job after we waited for about an hour. Carmella got so fed up after having me wait there with her, she told me to pull off and drive her home. As I was pulling out of the parking lot, Carmella said to me, "There his to late ass goes." I stopped the truck to let her talk to him as we pulled up right beside his little gold Honda Civic. She rolled down her window and said. "Really? Really?! This f--king late, Lenny?! No text, No call, No NOTHING!! You know what, you can keep going because I'm done with your Bullshit. I'm not getting out of this truck to get poured on by this rain… just to get in your dumb ass car. I'm going to the house and Ty is going to take me there, byyye!" She rolled her window back up before he could get a word out, told me to pull off and take her home.

I did just that. The ride to her house was pretty quiet for a bit, I could tell she had gotten furiously upset all over again after seeing Lenny. "Are you okay, Mella?" I asked.

"Yeah, I'm okay Ty. I'm just trying to control my emotions and not take it out on you in any kind of way because I really see that you care for me. I'm just done with that bastard!" She said with a tiredness look on her face, an ache behind her eyes, I had never seen there before.

"I know it, love; and I do really care for you... a lot, a lot! You think I would be out here in this pouring rain with you if I didn't? Hell nah!" We both laughed. "Nah; but all jokes to the side, I want you to understand that no matter what... I will always be there for you because I love you genuinely, wholeheartedly. I love everything about you, Mella. I love your hair and the way it smells like lavender. I love your skin tone; all I can think of is honey to compare it to. I love your dreamy beautiful eyes; I sometimes get lost in them. I see the hurt/pain inside of them and I want to be the one to help you dry those hidden tears up. I love your cute little dimples when you smile. I love your whole body, every curve of it is banging! Shaped like the curvy 8" She blushed and I flashed a brief smile her way. "I love your personality and I especially love the way you dance with me. I always think about you, I can't get you off of my mind and I have an extremely deep crush on you which is one of the reasons why I'm here right now with you." I said as I was now parked in front of her mother's apartment building. "I've been in love with you ever since we first laid eyes on each other years ago at that BBQ your aunt through back in the day. I said to her with a serious look on my face.

"Wow; that was so heartfelt, Ty. For real, I never really thought it was that deep but then again, I always knew because of our times when we kissed. I just didn't think that you liked me like that. I mean, I had some speculations but I never really knew it was that deep, Ty. That just touched my whole heart; but I have a confession to make to you now. Since you really told me how you feel about me, I have to tell you how I feel about you. I like you a lot too and I have a crush on you as well, Ty. I've been feeling this way for a long time now, all the way back when you gave me that first birthday present with the rap song you made up for me. I was like this is really dope!! That really meant a lot to me because I could tell you put time into wanting to make me happy and smile. You thought of me in a special way no other man has ever done before, that liked me or has ever been with me. The only reason why I never told you or acted on my like for you is because number 1, I was in a relationship with this asshole Lenny; and number 2, to tell you the truth I was scared. I was scared because I would have these thoughts of being with you and scared of what people would think of us being together. To be honest, I never dated a black guy before but when you came around, I instantly gravitated to you because you are so charming. My whole family loves you and I do too." Carmella said with sincerity in her eyes.

Lenny pulled up beside my parked truck, on Carmella's side of the truck, beeping his horn hysterically. Carmella rolled down her window and yelled out, "WHAT?!"

"Are you coming? I'm about to park and go inside." Lenny said as if her little breakup speech was one he had heard too many times before to take seriously.
"I'll be fine. I'm talking to Tyrone for a second, you can go in. He'll see me inside." She told him.

Lenny rode off fast like he was angry or something. "Anyway, forget him." She spun right back around to finish our conversation like Lenny never mattered in the first place. "So, yeah; there you have it. now we both know how we feel about each other, right.?" Before I could get a word out to say what I was going to say back to her, she leaned over to where I was sitting and it happened again. She kissed me, deeply and passionately. She pulled away and looked me in the eyes; then leaned in and did it again. This time, I kissed her back, sliding the tip of my tongue gently across her lips and waiting for her to part them for me. When she did, I felt myself relax in a way I never allowed the other times. This woman had me.

She pulled away slowly. "I would kiss you more, but I know this jerk Lenny is around here lurking somewhere and I don't want to put you in the middle of what him and I have going on. But keep those kisses dear to your heart and tell me all about it tomorrow." She placed another kiss on my lips. "Oh, I also have an extra ticket for you and Joe. If y'all want to come see me graduate, just let me know." She hugged me tightly like it was the last time I was going to see her or something and kissed me one last time. Then she told me, "Thank you for everything." As she was getting ready to exit out of the truck, I told her to wait because it was still pouring outside. Luckily, my aunt always kept a big umbrella in the truck for times like this. I grabbed the umbrella, got out of the truck, went around her side and opened her door. I helped her out of the truck, holding the umbrella over her head and walked her up the apartment stairs right to the door. She smiled, gave me another hug and said "thank you, Ty" and whispered in my ear, "I love you". I told her to call my phone soon as she made it safely in her home and then I would pull off and go about my business. I watched her walk in and go up the stairs, then she disappeared.

As I turned around, I saw Lenny approaching the apartment stairs. My phone had started to ring as I was walking down the stairs, it was Carmella. I answered and talked very boldly, so that Lenny could hear me. "Hello?... Oh Okay, you made it in safe?... Okay good, call me if you ever need me for anything. You know I got you, Mella! Hahaaa, anytime love, okay, you too... Good night"

Lenny and I looked each other in the face as we crossed paths on the stairs but didn't say a word to each other. He went inside pissed off and I got into my truck. I waited five minutes, just in case Mella called me back and I had to go upstairs to her apartment and whoop Lenny's ass; but she never called, so I just rode off.

Chapter *12*

The Fight/ Graduation Day

After the day that I sat hours in the stormy rain with Carmella in my truck waiting for her sorry excuse for a boyfriend to come pick her up, she and I started becoming really close more. I was going over her mother's apartment more often than normal and I also began to pick her up from work, most night's she had to work because she was tired of depending on Lenny to do so. Boy, was he mad!! My plan to make Carmella my wife was starting to look up and all I was doing was showing up when she needed me to and being just simply being real with her. That was a really big deal to Carmella. All she wanted was someone to show her that they cared about her; someone to show her that she meant something to them, someone loyal and I was that guy that was doing that.

Eventually, she got rid of Lenny. He really pissed me and her off one night and that was her last straw with him. This particular night, Joe and I had gotten invited to one of Carmella's family parties like we always did in the past. Every time Joe and I showed up to these family functions, we were the life of the party because everyone loved how we danced. Carmella's whole family loved Joe and I but we knew some of the other guys that were there were hating on us. We didn't care though; we were dancing with their girls and the girls were loving it. Lenny was one of the main haters there. He hated to see Carmella and I dancing because when we danced, it would not only be to one song. It would be to several. Back to back to back to back, etc. Everyone knew Carmella loved to dance with me and vice versa. Plus, Lenny never ever danced with Carmella at any parties I ever went to. So, I guess he wasn't a dancer; but I sure was.

Anyway, Carmella and I were on the floor dancing. It must have been like the third bachata song getting ready to mix right in from the last one that was playing. The song that came on was from an artist named "Yoskar Sarante" and the title of his song was, "Tu el y yo". It was a very popular Spanish song at the time and the Dominican people loved to dance to it. As the song began to play, Carmella and I moved in closer to each other and started dancing in a very erotic manner. When we danced, I swear it always felt like just her and I were the only ones there on the dance floor... but that wasn't reality. We were dancing in front of a house full of her family as well as her boyfriend Lenny, who everyone could tell was sitting on the couch hotter than a summer day in Miami. Every time I spun Carmella around and looked at Lenny, I could see his face get redder and steam coming from out of his ears. Finally, he couldn't take it no more. He got up from his chair, walked right over to where Carmella and I were dancing and said, "Mella, I'm about to get out of here." Carmella looked at him and simply just said, "Ok Bye". It was like she didn't even care that he was leaving. It sort of felt like she was happy he was leaving. Lenny walked out of the door and everybody continued dancing; not a single beat was skipped.

Carmella, looked at me, smiled, put the right side of her face on my chest and continued to dance with me. All of a sudden, Lenny comes back into the house in a very disrespect manner. He started screaming at Mella saying to her, "So, you don't care if I'm leaving now!? You don't care where I'm going!? FINE! Stay here and continue to dance with this BLACK NIGGA Motherfucker!" Everybody was in total shock at the racial remark Lenny just spat out... especially Carmella.

"What did you just say to me, Bitch?!" I angrily yelled back at Lenny while getting up in his face and before he could get out the rest of his words, I snapped. I lunged at him to try and punch him in his face but I was grabbed and pulled back by Joe as Carmella's family members scrambled in between us, pushing, shoving and screaming at Lenny to get out of their home. They did not like what he said at all and they let it be known quickly.

Downstairs, Lenny was acting like he didn't want to leave from in front of their house, so I somehow got loose from Joe holding me, ran outside to attack him again and was stopped by some of the family members. Lenny finally got the picture that I wanted to beat his face in badly after the second time I lunged at him and was going to stop at nothing until I got to do just that. I even punched the wood light pole a few times to let him know pain didn't matter to me. [My hand paid for that through the next couple of weeks.] So, he immediately got into his car and I sped off quickly. I was in such a fit of a rage outside of Carmella's family home that I even stupidly punched the wooden electricity pole. That was very dumb, but I didn't care at the time. I just wanted that to be Lenny's head I was punching for what he had said to me.

Nobody was able to calm my nerves for a while. I mean, I really felt disrespected by what Luis had said about me in front of all those people and especially being the only black person in there. I felt at the time. Later I come to find out Mella family didn't just snap because he said a racist remark to me only but to them as well. See, in some of the Spanish culture, some of the people forget that they're African decent which makes them Afro-Latino but Mella family knew and was not tolerating it at all. Joe's family taught me that a long time ago as well. Joe's father's name was "Negro" which means "Black" in English. Anyway, my hand started to swell up from hitting the wooden electricity pole so much; so, I started to take a walk down the block. As I started to walk, I heard a sweet voice from behind me say, "Tyrone, hold on, I'm coming with you." It was Carmella. She grabbed my right arm with her left arm and said, "Where are you going? Are you okay? I'm so sorry about what that simpleton said to you. Ughh!! I'm so done with him!! But… But my main concern is you now. I want to know… are you okay, Ty?"

We got to the corner at the end of the block, it was a little distance from where her family's house was; but you could still see us from there. Carmella's family watch us from a distance as we continued to talk. "I'm fine, love. I don't know about your man, though or your ex or whatever. He's real lucky I didn't get to him. I would have taken his head off!" I screamed; then I realized who I was talking to. I'm sorry, Mella. It's just that I want to know what is it? What is it that you see in guys like that? He's jealous, he doesn't care about you; you tell me this all the time. He's never on time to pick you up and that's if he ever shows up to get you at all. What is it? Do you like being done dirty?"

Carmella just looked at me with tears in her eyes and said, "I don't know Ty. I don't know why I allow this to happen to myself but not anymore. I'm done with him, I'm Done!!" She yelled, bursting into tears. "He makes me sick and what he did and said tonight was very unacceptable. I care about you, Tyrone, I love the way you treat me, how you are always there for me and for him to say such nasty things towards you, I won't allow it! I mean, look at your hand, it's swollen!" We both giggled. "Why in the world would you hit the damn electric pole?" She asked me.

"I was heated. I wanted to knock his head off of his shoulders; but I apologize for acting so crazy in front of you and your family, I really didn't want them to see that side of me ever but old boy definitely pushed that button. I'm sorry though, Mella. Are you mad at me?" I asked her looking into her eyes like a lost puppy.

She put both of her arms around my back, looked me in the eyes, kissed me on my lips, pulled back and said, "No Tyrone, I'm not mad at you at all. How can I be? I'm pissed at him but I'm not mad at you at all. It actually was kind of cute seeing you pop off the way you did." We both giggled and kissed each other again. "Come on we better get back to the party, I know my nosy family is up there watching and probably worried about if we're okay; but I just want to tell you thank you." She said as we started walking back up the block.

"For what?" I asked, confused.

"Thank you for being you and opening up my eyes tonight on a lot of things." She said looking away.

"You're welcome, Carmella; but you still can't see me on that dance floor. I don't care what you say. Thank me for teaching you some new moves in bachata, thank me for that." I said as we both laughed, walking each other back up to her family's home.

Two weeks went by after that drama filled night with myself almost having to knock Lenny's head off his shoulders. Joe woke me up out of my sleep early this Friday morning. It was about 7am. "Yo Ty, get up, bro. Get up, man. I just got off the phone with Sariah and she asked if we were going to Mella graduation. We're going, right?" Joe said, aggressively shoving my body to wake me up.

"Hell yeah, we're going! What time does it start?" I asked, immediately popping up from my bed.

"It starts at 8:30am; so, let's get up, get dressed and get down there now because it's already 7am!" Joe said as we both rushed to get ourselves in order to make it down to Carmella high school on time to see her walk across the stage.

Even though she told me a while back that she had some tickets for us to attend, she had no clue I was going to actually be there. This meant a lot to me, showing up to see Carmella graduate from high school. I felt like it was always my duty to be at anything that meant something to her. I just wanted to always show her that I would be there no matter what and that I was a constant consistent loyal person in her life, that loved her dearly.

There were so many people at Carmella's high school when Joe and I arrived. Luckily, we found parking right around the block from the high school, in front of a corner bodega and walked from there. As Joe and I were approaching the school, we were greeted by Carmella's mother and sisters. I didn't see Sariah. Joe said she would be showing up later. Carmella's mother was so happy to see Joe and I. She gave us each tight hugs and cheek kisses, then handed us tickets to enter the school as we all got on the long line. We finally got in and proceeded to take our seats in the school's auditorium after about 20 minutes.

Carmella's mother was so happy and excited that I was there, she wanted me to sit next to her. So, I did. I was super excited and happy as well. They started calling out all of the graduate's names as they walked on the stage to shake the principal's hand and receive their diplomas. There were so many students there. They were calling names forever. They finally got to the letter "M" and her mother stood up.

Carmella was up next... "Carmella Mendoza" the person over the loud speaker said and all I remember was basically the whole auditorium making hella noise right alongside with us when her name was called. I felt so proud of her at that moment; I felt like I was the one receiving my diploma all over again. I could tell she had a lot of love in that school because people clapped and cheered for her like we were at a concert. It was so amazing.

After it was all over, everybody waited outside of the school for the graduates to come out to greet their families and the people who came to see them graduate. By this time, there were a lot more family members and friends waiting for Carmella to come out of the school. "CONGRATULATIONS!!" Everyone screamed out as Carmella walked out to greet all of us.

"THANK YOU! THANK YOU!!" She said to everyone, giving us all hugs and kisses. A lot of us brought her gifts, balloons and Roses. She was so amazed at all the love she was receiving. She had the biggest prettiest smile on her face. As she was greeting everyone who was there for her, she hadn't noticed Joe and I yet because we played the background to let her intermediate family greet her first.

As Joe and I started walking up to her, she jetted over to us and said, "Tyrone, Joe, thanks for coming! Ty, I didn't even know you were here, y'all just made my day that more special!"

I handed her some flowers with a card and a gift and said, "Congratulations, Mella. I'm so very proud of you and of course I'm here. I wouldn't have missed this for the world."

She smiled and gave me another hug and then a quick kiss and said, "Thank you so much."

Joe and I stayed for another 10 minutes; then we told Carmella and her family we had to go handle some business and that we'd see them later. The family hugged and kissed us and said "ok". We walked off with the very good feeling that we left another great impression on them. Especially, after that crazy night when I was about to fight Lenny. I didn't want to leave her family with the impression of me as a bad taste of me in their mouths. So, I was very happy that we had made it to Carmella's graduation.

A whole year went by after that day and I was getting ready for my second year in college. I would go see Carmella like every other week after she graduated for that whole year. During this same time, I had linked up with a few older heads that I used to do music with and sell drugs on the streets with. Growing up in the hood, even though you try to do right, wrong is always right around the corner. I eventually fell victim to the streets and played my part in it. I was easily hypnotized and drawn in by how much money those older guys would always have. I saw how fast they were getting it too. The life of a hustler was so romanticized that my decision to get into those streets and make money was a no-brainer.

I got my own package of marijuana/weed and started hustling for myself right out the gate. I also sold cocaine and ecstasy pills at some point. I had a job at the college as well; but it was only part time and it wasn't paying much money at all. I needed more money to do the things that I wanted to do... like buy Carmella the nice things I wanted her to have. Plus, I knew there were other guys with money trying to get at her too in the area where she lived. I knew I had competition, especially with her being as fine as she was. I had to have money at all times; and after a short while, I was getting it, heavy.

One day, I stopped by Carmella's job to pick her up from work. This time, she was getting off early in the afternoon. I remember this day like it was yesterday. It was a Saturday afternoon at around 4pm. I picked her up from her job and she was happy as ever to see me. As I rode us to her apartment, I asked, "Yo Mella, what are you doing with your life? Is this it? You just want to work at One State your whole life or do you want more and better for it?"

She looked at me with a blank stare on her face like she was shocked I even asked. "Umm, no... I hate that freaking job; but I don't know what I want to do with my life right this second. Ever since I graduated from high school, I've been asking myself the same thing and I haven't come up with anything as of yet. So, I do not know yet but I know I want to do something more than this!" Carmella said letting out a sigh of frustration immediately after.

"That's it!! You're coming to school with me! I told you my sister's in admissions and I'm going to get you into college Mella." I said, feeling like I needed to make the decision for her.

"WHAT! Oh, I don't know about college, Ty. I mean, I never even thought of going to college. I don't even have the money to pay for it." She said, her face riddled with indecisiveness.

"Look, don't worry about that. You can get financial aid and you probably can even get your own dorm room under that financial aid plan. I'm telling you; this will be great for you Mella. Something new; a restart from just working at One State Supermarket. You'll be able to meet new people, create new opportunities for yourself, and you'll be getting more educated at the same time. Look, I will even come pick you up from your home and take you up there, introduce you to my sister, tell her to do everything for you to get you started and we will take it from there. I'll let her know." I said excitingly to her.

"Well, it is starting to sound a little more exciting to me now that you put it that way." She looked off into the distance as she thought it over. "Okay, fine. When do you want to take me up to the college?" Carmella asked with a smile.

"Tomorrow!! I'll call my sister in a few and let her know we're coming in tomorrow." I said eagerly.

"Tomorrow?!" She yelled back at me.

"Yes, tomorrow!! Look Mella, there's no reason to procrastinate on this. This is for your future; you will not regret this, trust me. Plus, imagine your family's faces when you tell them that you're going to college. Everyone will be in shock but very proud of you, especially your mom. I know it! So, I'll be here to get you at 9:30am. Be prepared to spend most of the day at the college, okay?" I said to her, loving the light growing behind her eyes the more we talk about it.

"Okay, cool. I'll be ready at 9:30am. Thanks Ty, I'm like super excited now." She smiled hard, showing how deep her dimples really were.

I won't lie, that smile and those dimples made my day. The more I got to see her happy, the more I wanted to be the reason she felt that way.

Chapter *13*

College/Bad News/Prison

It was 9:30am on a beautiful sunny Friday morning in June of 2001. I was just pulling up to Carmella apartment building to pick her up and take her to New Jersey City University to get her registered in. I called her phone and told her to come on downstairs. I was waiting parked outside of her apartment. About 10 minutes went by with me just sitting in my black Range Rover, listening to Hot 97 play music on the radio. All I could think to myself was, *where in the world is Carmella, it shouldn't take this long for her to come out.* Just as I was about to turn the truck off and go find out what was taking her so long, I heard the front door to the apartment building open and saw this gorgeous woman come out of the building. It was Carmella. Her in a sundress seemed like the reason the sun had risen bright that day. She had definitely just washed her hair because it was hanging in wet curls and bouncing off her buttocks as she walked down her apartment building steps. I just looked at her in awe, mesmerized at how gorgeous she was.

"What's up, Ty! Why you smiling so hard?" She said, walking around to get in on the passenger side of my truck.

"I'm smiling so hard because I'm happy you're going through with getting yourself into college and you look fine as ever too!" I said as I let my eyes take more and more of her in the closer, she got to getting inside of the truck. She got in and closed the door. She anxiously leaned into give me a kiss and her perfume danced around in my nostrils.

I drove off and on the way to the University, we conversed. She told me how nervous she was because she had never even considered going to college. She also told me how proud her mother was of her; and how thankful she was for me doing this for her daughter. I was just happy to have the privilege of making her happy.

We pulled up to the University's parking lot and I parked the truck in one of the open spaces. We got out of the truck and we proceeded to walk towards where my sister's building and office were. The campus was beautiful; students were laying in study groups in the shade of big trees, a line of sorority pledges marched past us singing, every face that passed us was smiling. It was like I had picked the perfect day to bring her to the university because the campus was showing off for us. We got to my sister's office and the secretary alerted my sister that Carmella and I were out in the waiting area. She came out immediately. "TY!? Hey honey. How are..." She greeted me with a huge hug. "And this must be the gorgeous lady, Carmella you've been telling me about!! Hello sweetheart, happy to have you here!! Come into my office so we can get everything discussed and handled." My sister properly greeted us like I already knew she would. She had a soulful joy about herself, no one could resist her charm. Carmella nerves were automatically comforted by my sister's genuine excitement to help her be at ease and comfort.

We all entered my sister's office and sat down. "So... Como tú estas Carmella, Dimelo?" My sister asked Carmella in Spanish, it meant, 'How are you doing Carmella; talk to me" in English.

"Oh my goodness, you speak Spanish too? That is so dope! You have like the coolest sister, Tyrone." Carmella said feeling visibly at ease.

"Thanks. Isn't she dope, Mella!" I said, winking at my older sister. "Anyway, Tam, I would like for you to get Carmella registered in for a semester of school here. Can you hook it up?" I got right to business.

"I sure can! Tell you what Carmella, I'm going to set you up with the basic classes every freshman starts out with here and then we'll go from there. Deal?" My sister asked Carmella.

"Okay, yes. Of course, it's a deal. I just want to tell you both, thank you for giving me this opportunity. I never thought in a million years I'd be going to college. I only have one question, how much do these classes cost and how will I go about paying for them because I know going to college is expensive." Carmella got straight to the point.

"Great question, girl!! Okay, so after I set up everything as far as your classes, Tyrone will take you to where they handle financial aid. You will go down there and give them all the information they ask you for, to see if you qualify for it. More than likely you will; then there it is... you're in. As long as you don't fall behind by failing your classes, you will be able to get financial aid to help you pay for all of your classes. They'll explain everything to you on how it works, when you go there. Any other questions, please feel free to ask me?" My sister explained.

"How many classes will I have this first semester?" Carmella's nerves reared their fuming heads again.

"Six, but don't worry, any student coming straight out of high school can carry the load." My sister assured her.

"What about the dorm rooms?"

"Financial aid will cover that as well. Again, they will break all that down to you in their office. Anything else?" My sister smiled as she typed super-fast without looking away from us for more than a second or two at a time.

"Nope, I'll ask them anything else that comes to mind that I need to know once I get to that office. Thank you so much again, Mrs. Tammy!" Carmella said with sincerity in her eyes.

"Great!! I have another meeting very shortly. So, here are your classes. Take this to financial aid and here are two free lunch passes to get whatever you two beautiful souls want to eat at our cafeteria here on campus. Ty, take this lovely lady to lunch when y'all are through with financial aid. Thank you both for stopping by and I'm so very happy to meet you and also to have you enrolled with us, Carmella." My sister, guiding us back out of her office with a smile.

We both thanked her and proceeded to the financial aid office as she insisted us to do. We handled the financial aid part of it all and Carmella was officially registered to attend the University for next semester which was two months away.

As we walked out of the financial aid building, I asked her, "Are you hungry because I'm STARVING?"

She giggled. "Yes, I am too!"

"Let's go use these damn free cafeteria passes my sister gave to us then." I held my arm out for her to take hold of it. She did.

"Let's do it!" She placed her hand in the crook of my arm and let me lead the way.

I could tell she was extra happy that she had gotten registered. I saw the excitement all over her face when we were sitting in the cafeteria eating. We both got two chicken wraps and they were Banging! After that, I showed Carmella around the entire campus. I took her to where the freshman classes were held, to the large park where everyone studied and hung out between classes, and we even stopped at one spot they did open mic on campus. I took her to the library, the game room, and two of the Fraternity/Sorority houses where a few of my friends and I would party often. I also took her to the gymnasium, where all the basketball and volleyball games were held. I showed her where the pool and weight room were, just in case she wanting to keep that firm body of hers in shape. It was starting to get late in the evening and I had a few things to do (like go reup on a package of marijuana in New York City). So, I asked her if she was ready to head back home and she said "yes".

We walked towards the parking lot, got into the truck, and drove off. The whole ride to her house, Carmella could not stop talking about how happy and thankful she was for me making her go to college and get registered. I finally pulled up to her apartment building and said "I'm really proud of you, punk. You're going to do great things and if you ever need any help with your classes, just ask me and I got you."

She just looked at me for about ten seconds after I said that. Then she took her seatbelt off, leaned over to where I was sitting, put her right hand on top of my pants where my "daddy long stroke" was and caressed it as our lips locked in passion. She said, "I sure will and thank you so much for always caring about me and being there for me, Tyrone. I really do appreciate you, for real. The way I feel about you is indescribable and I love it. Have a good night and call me when you make it home safely, okay." She got out of the truck and went up the stairs to the front door of her apartment building. Then she turned around when she got to the top, took a look back, waved bye to me and said it again softly through the air, "I love you" and walked inside the building.

I rode off just enough to be out of eyesight from the front door. With the windows up, I screamed at the top of my lungs, "YESSSS!!! I LOVE YOUUUU MELLA!!" I thought to myself, *I finally got her on my side, I finally got the girl I always wanted to be with. I finally got the girl of my dreams, the one who I always had a crush on. The one who I said I was going to make my wife.* I was so ecstatic; I couldn't wait to tell my brother Joe the great news.

After that beautiful Friday, another 2 months passed by and the new semester was here; but there was only one problem. I hadn't seen or heard from Carmella at all. I got really busy out there in the streets and preparing myself for the first semester classes, so I hadn't been talking to her at all.

I tried to call her a few times but I never got to speak to her. I left a couple of messages for her to call me back, but she never did. I even stopped by her job numerous of times and never saw her there.

The first day of the new semester came and Carmella was nowhere to be found. I was starting to get worried about where she could be. So, after my last class for the day, I went down to her mother's apartment and tried to see if I could reach her there. I got nothing. I was really disappointed and worried about her. I just really wanted to know if she was safe because I couldn't understand how she was so excited to be going to college two months ago and now she's become a no-show. *How did no one know where she was?*

She was nowhere to be found for about two more months after the semester started. I often wondered about her but continued on with my life. Besides being back in college, I was hustling a lot of weight. Mainly marijuana; but also, a little ecstasy and cocaine as I stated earlier. I was living a double life. In the day time, I was at school. At night, I was hustling up extra money for myself.

Like anyone who's ever seen any hood film could have predicted, the streets started to take a real toll on my life. I wasn't doing the best in my classes anymore. After I started making heavy money on the streets, school didn't really matter as much as it used to once before. I wish I didn't think like that at the time; I wish I had finished school but the money got in the way of my vision and purpose.

I was still best friends with my brother Joe though. His parents used to let me stay in the basement of their house and that's where I wrote most of my music and raps. I was turning myself into a rap artist at that time as well. I always saw myself performing on big stages in front of millions of people. I wrote my first rhyme when I was 7-years-old and I loved making music ever since then. I was determined to make something of that dream.

One day, I was down in the basement, writing a rap to an instrumental beat and Joe came in from chilling at Sariah's house. He said he had to talk to me and that it was pretty urgent concerning Carmella. My heart automatically skipped a beat and my stomach got a knot in it. I thought the worst because I hadn't heard from her in a whole three months.

Joe turned down the music that was playing on the speaker and asked, "Bro, when was the last time you heard from or saw Mella?"

I immediately responded, "The last time I saw her was the day I got her registered for school with my sister. After that, I haven't seen or heard from her for about 4 months now, bro. You know that. Why, what's up man? Is she okay? Did you get to ask Sariah about her? What's going on?" I was rambling already because his question alone left me so concerned.

I knew there was something wrong by the way Joe was acting. "Yeah, I know bro. Well, I did ask Sariah what's been up with her and she told me that she's okay and the reason why she has disappeared is because she is pregnant bro and it's not by Lenny either. It's by some new guy, I think he's Puerto Rican or something. Sariah said there's something going on with that whole story though because the guy is in a suicide watch facility. Apparently, he tried to throw himself off a bridge. I don't know, bro. Something is very strange about the whole thing to me." He shook his head and I could see in his eyes that he knew how deeply the news had struck me.

My heart sank. *Pregnant? How could she be pregnant? Who the hell was this new guy?* I was so devastated; but in some weird way, I was happy Carmella was at least safe. "Wow, so it's not with Lenny? She was with some other guy? Damn, she never mentioned anything about anyone else she was seeing and we used to talk about everything. She even gave me a kiss that day I got her registered for school. Now she's pregnant by a whole new guy and this guy is a sicko!!" I said it all out loud to make it more real. I just couldn't understand what I was hearing from Joe. "I guess that's the reason why she never showed up to school. Damn man, I got to see her. Something still doesn't sound right." I said as I stared at the floor between us.

"I feel you, bro. Something does still seem a little off. I want to know why dude is in the suicide place. That's strange; and then everybody in her family saying she been all to herself lately." Joe added.

"As soon as I see her, I will get to the bottom of everything because whatever she is going through, I just want her to know that I will always be there for her... if she allows me to." I told my brother.

Joe turned the music back up and said, "Enough of that for now. Let me hear that new hotness you been writing." I spit some hot bars for him the whole rest of the night, but Carmella never left my mind for a second.

About six months went by after that day and I still hadn't seen or heard anything from Carmella yet. I got so caught up in the streets that she wasn't really a main topic on my brain anymore, but she was always a faint thought in the back of my mind. I knew some people that knew some people, that knew Carmella. These people also knew about the guy who had gotten her pregnant. What I heard from these people that I knew about what really happened to Carmella was some really devastating news to me. It really hurt my soul! I wanted to find that dude who got her pregnant and hurt him really, really, badly.

Someone told me, Carmella felt really sick one day and was throwing up all over the place for a few days and felt that she needed to go to the hospital because it was becoming unbearable. She went to the hospital and told the doctors she wanted to take a pregnancy test because she had recently slept with a guy unprotected and she thought she might be pregnant. The doctors gave her a pregnancy test and came to find out that she was right, she was pregnant. The doctors ask if she planned on keeping the baby and said that if she was, she should let them run more test on her to make sure she was healthy enough for the pregnancy. Carmella gave the doctors the "ok" to run more tests. After running all the rest of the tests on her, the doctors came back into the room Carmella was in and told her the worst news she ever probably heard in her life. They told her that not only was she four months pregnant but that she was also HIV positive. This is what my sources told me; To me, it was all hear-say and speculation, something I did not want to believe for her sake. Still, the possibility that it was true was enough for me.

When I heard that terrible news about Carmella, it just CRUSHED ME!! My spirit was destroyed. All I wanted was the best for Carmella, ever since I laid eyes on her. I never in a million years would have imagined this devastating news of her contracting HIV to be a real thing; but this was the news. I didn't know what to think anymore, I just needed to see her. To talk to her and let her know I was still going to be there for her if this bad news was true.

After hearing what I heard, months went by and I went on with my life. Still hustling out on the streets and making major moves. It was 7:30 PM this one particular Friday night. I was outside running the streets of Jersey City. Hanging with my street homies, hustling like I normally did. I told the homies I was going to the liquor store to buy all of us a big bottle of Hennessy. I usually did that after having a good week of hustling hard. So, I went to the liquor store and it was pretty packed in there with a few people I knew from other blocks in my hood. I was standing on line talking to those people and waiting on my turn to get to the register when all of a sudden, I recognized a sweet voice come from behind me so gently and say, "Ty?" I ignored the person calling out my government name at first because no one knew me by it anymore. I had an alias; everyone called me BLAK and had for a while. So, hearing "Ty" was foreign to me and then the voice called out my name again, this time more firmly. "Ty? Tyrone!?" I couldn't ignore it anymore. I realized this had to be a person that knew me for a long time. So, I turned around to see who it was calling my government name out like that. As soon as I turned around, I saw a Spanish female with her head covered with an army fatigue cap over her head. I couldn't really see her face, so I grabbed the brim of the cap and tilted it up a little. I could not believe who was standing in front of me.

"MELLA!! Is that really you!? Where in the world have you been!? What are you doing all the way over here at this time of night!?" She had lost some of the magnifying glow I once remembered her to always have but even the dulled down version of her couldn't take away from her beauty that shined from within. She still looked very gorgeous though.

She just looked at me with the biggest smile on her face and said "Oh my God, I can't believe it's you, Tyrone. I heard you speaking over there with those two guys and I said that guy looks a lot like Tyrone. How have you been!? I'm so sorry for going M.I.A. I have so much to tell you, but not here. I just moved into my new apartment on Sip Avenue and Westside, what are you doing tonight? You should stop by and come hang with me, so we could catch up some." She seemed so excited to see me, but I still had those thoughts of what I heard about her health status on my mind.

"Most definitely! I'll get us a bottle and bring it over to your apartment. We definitely have to catch up on a lot because I want to know where the hell you went? Text my phone your address now and I'll be over shortly." I said to her, trying my best not to be obvious as my eyes examined the rest of her. Could I tell just by looking at her? I would know, right? I don't know but I would find out and then tell her, it's okay, I still got her back and still love her but I knew if this were to be true, I could no longer want to be with her. I took her phone and put my number into a blank text.

"Okay, that's cool with me." She took my phone and sent the text. "I just sent you my address, check and see if you got my text. Oh yeah and about what I'm doing here... I needed to get some dutches. Do you know where I can get some smoke?" She whispered as if she didn't want anyone else to hear her ask that question.

"Absolutely!! I got a whole wop of some in my pocket right now! Tell you what, I got your address in my phone, let me go drop this off to my peoples on my block and I'm heading right over to you. Give me like...

20 minutes. I got you on everything. Cool?" I said, noticing how much I had changed. I wasn't that eager young dude I used to be for her ever since the last time I had seen her. I was more at ease in my own skin. A lot had changed. I felt heartbroken when she disappeared from me, out of nowhere. So, I still had a litter hesitant resentment towards her. I was crushed about what I heard about her and disappointed I might not ever get the chance to show her I wanted her to be my wife.

"Ok, that's cool. Thank you, Ty; and make sure you come through. Okay?" She said with a big smile. "I'm coming, promise" I said back.

We both got what we came into the liquor store for and left out together.

Chapter *14*

Last Time Seeing Each Other

After dropping one of the two liquor bottles off to my homies on my block, I headed straight to Carmella's place. It took me about 15 minutes to get to her block. The text she sent me said, "219 Sip Avenue, ring apt 3". I approached her building and saw all the bells on the side of the building door. I found the bell labeled "apt 3" and rung it. Just a few seconds after, I heard a voice yell, "Who's that?" It sounded like Carmella voice through the little black speaker.

"It's Ty, Mella." I answered back.

"Okay, I'm about to buzz you in. Come to the third floor." She responded.

BZZZZZZZ!! I heard the buzzer click to let open the door. So, I pushed the metal and glass door forward and proceeded into the apartment building. As I was walking up the stairs about to hit the third floor, I looked up and saw this gorgeous woman standing outside of her apartment door with the biggest smile on her face. It was Carmella. I finally got to her door and said to her, "Y'all need an elevator."

She laughed at me and said, "For real! Come in though. I'm so happy you really came, Ty!"

"What you thought I wasn't going to come or something? Now when do you know me for not keeping my word, Mella? And I brought this and that too." I said, putting a bottle of Hennessy on her living room table, along with a bag full of weed.

She was extra excited when she saw all of the weed I brought! "DAMNNNNN! That's a lot of weed, Ty! I'm going to be calling to buy some off of you from now on, so I don't have to deal with no one else when I want to cop some. Is that cool?" She asked.

"Of course, love. I'll always come through and hook you up; you know I got you. I'll even smoke one with you each time you call me. How's that?" I looked around. "So, this is your new place, huh? I like it… it's nice and cozy." I said as we both sat down on her comfortable living room sofa.

As I took one of the Dutch Masters she had on her living room table in front of us, I started rolling some of the weed up in it. All of a sudden, I heard what seemed to be the sound of a cat crying coming from one of the bedrooms. At this point, Carmella had turned on some music and played it at a low volume, but I still kept hearing what I thought was a cat crying. So, I asked, "Mella, you got a cat in one of your rooms or something? What's that crying sound?"

"Oh no, I forgot you don't know yet? Come here with me for a second." She grabbed my hand and pulled me towards one of her bedrooms. Then told me to wait by the door. She went into her room for about 30 seconds and came back out with a whole new born baby and that's when it hit me. This was the baby her cousin Sariah told Joe about that she had with the insane guy who tried to commit suicide because he allegedly gave her HIV and went to the crazy house. "Ty, this is the reason I didn't come back to school. This is my daughter, Angel. After that day I went to school with you, got registered and had such a fun day on campus with you, I had a doctor's appointment a few days after. I wasn't feeling to well at the time you took me to get registered for school but I went because I loved how you always wanted to see better for me in life. I really wanted to go to school with you; but when I went to that doctor's appointment, I found out I was four months pregnant with Angel. I was so crushed because I knew that it would crush you, since we were really starting to feel each other as more than friends. I didn't know what to do; I was completely mad at myself because I didn't want to be with the guy I had slept with. I wanted to be with you; but I was dealing with him before we started to really reveal our feelings for one another." A sad look came over her face for a few seconds.

"Wow, she is beautiful Mella! I never knew that was what happened to you but now it's all starting to make sense. Thank you for showing me her and God bless her." I said to Carmella as she walked back into the room to lay her baby Angel back down to sleep in her crib. She came back out of the room, closed the door and said to me, "Let's Smoke Negro!"

We both giggled at each other going back into her living room. As I sat down on her maroon leather sofa, I grabbed the weed from off of the table in front of me and started to break it up to put inside of the weed leaf.

"What do you want to listen to?" Carmella asked.

"Here pop this in your sound system." I said, handing her my newly finished mixtape CD. It was titled "More Focused Than Eva" and it had the streets buzzing all over Jersey City at the time. She put my mixtape in her CD player and told me she wanted to go outside on her balcony to smoke because she didn't want to smoke inside with her baby in the house. I respected that she was concerned about her baby's well-being, so we went on the balcony which was cool because we could still hear the music while we smoked and talked. I took a long pull of the weed, inhaled it, then passed her the joint. I could tell the conversation was about to get really deep as she was bopping her head, really feeling the vibe of my music.

"Yo Ty, this is really good stuff. You always been nice with the music. I still have that tape you gave to me as a part of my present that one year for my birthday. That was so special to me." She looked up at the night sky. "You know I never really meant to disappear from you, Tyrone. I just had a lot going on at the time and things got very overwhelming for me.

You know, finding out I was about to be a mother was hard in itself, especially by a guy that I wasn't going to be with. He just ruined my whole life and plans I had going forward with you. I was so hurt by it and I didn't know how to tell you, so I ran away from you. I'm so sorry for that because you have always been there for me and always loved me and I just want to tell you thank you so much for that. When I realized all of what had happened, I knew it would probably crush you because I knew how deep your feelings were for me. I knew how everything was starting to be with us. I just didn't want to hurt you. So, the next best thing I knew to do was avoid you; but when I saw you in the liquor store just now, hearing you talk just brought back so many great memories I have in my head of you. I need that so much right now." Carmella said as I started to see her eyes get very watery. She looked and sounded like she wanted to tell me something so badly but she was a little nervous or afraid to let it out.

"It's okay, Mella. I'm not mad at you at all. I just want you to know that as long as you and I are breathing and we are in touch with each other, I will always be there for you. I am not mad that you have your baby at all, Mella. I'm mad at the things I heard about this guy when I went looking for you. I heard he's in a mental facility because he was going to jump off a bridge. Where and how did you meet this sicko? What made you mess with him if you didn't want to mess with him. I heard terrible things and I'm not going to say anymore of what I've heard… but just know I've heard and I do know." I paused to inhale some weed. "Look where I'm at, still here for you. Why, because God has put me here as one of the people who genuinely loves you. I'm going to always be there for you, Mella. No matter what. One day in the future, I'm going to sit down and write a book about all the times I've spent with you and how you made me feel just being in your presence. That's how much I love you, I'm going to write a freaking book about it. Watch you'll see!!" I said as she smiled at me.

"You see, that right there, is the thing that I love so much about you. You are so different from anyone I've ever known or have ever dated. To tell you the truth Tyrone, I wish I never messed with none of these guys. None of them. I wish you and I laid eyes on each other first and I fell madly in love with you. I met the father of my child walking home from work one day because once again Lenny didn't come pick me up like he said he was going to. I was so fed up with him, plus our relationship was practically over. Anyway, I met him walking home and we started to see each other and hang out from time to time. We never did anything nasty until one time I was feeling vulnerable because I had just gotten into a huge argument with Lenny again, after I found out he was cheating on me with someone yet again. Now that I think about it all, I shouldn't have even cared. I should have just dump Lenny' wack ass and moved on with my life; but what does Carmella do? Sleep with a random guy I just met and get pregnant. The guy was so nice at first but when I went to take the pregnancy test and found out I was pregnant; I knew I had to go see the doctor. He just went totally crazy on me. He started doing a lot of crazy stuff, like he had a bad batch of drugs or something. I couldn't understand why at the time but I do now and it sounds like you know why too." A single tear cascaded down her cheek. "I was so hurt, Tyrone and so mad at myself because I didn't want this. I feel so alone, so uneasy about this whole situation. So, when I saw you in that liquor store, it made me feel so good because you've always done that for me. You've always put my nerves or problems to rest and I so need that right now."

I could see the hurt all over her. She was scared and I was feeling very sad for her because this was the woman I truly loved and cared about. This was the woman I once knew would be the love of my life some day and she was telling me she was in pain. I never wanted any of this for this woman but what could I do... Except and be there for her. "I'm still going to be here for you, Mella. No matter what." We stepped inside from the balcony as I was getting calls from my customers. I needed to get back out there because I was missing money. Plus, I thought that I would just come chill with Mella and smoke her out a few blunts and leave her a big bag of weed. I knew where she lived now, so I knew it would be no problem for me to pop up and check on her. So, I told Carmella, "I got to be heading out now. It's already late as ever and I know you got your baby in there sleep. Plus, my phone is going crazy right now, it's booming out there. I got to make this money baby but look... I know where you are at now. I'll be coming through here frequently, just to check up on you and the baby, smoke you out and chill. If that's okay with you, of course. I know you need someone other than your family right now; so, I'll be that someone if you let me be and we can talk and just bond more like we used to do. Is that cool with you?"

She looked at me with this look of relief, like she was surprised and somewhat happy again. "Yes, please come through anytime, Ty. I want you to; I need you to. I don't know nobody around this area and I don't want to know anybody either. I just want to bond with you again. I love our bond; and yes, we do have to talk more about other things I want to tell and release to you for myself. Even though it sounds like you already know. I wouldn't mind you coming by at all, at any time. Promise me you will." Carmella said.

"Of course, I will, Mella You know I will. Come on now. Here, come here and give me a big hug." I opened my arms and she walked into them. When I squeezed her, I realized that she hadn't been the only one that needed the hug. "It's so good to finally have seen you again. I've missed you so much, woman. Don't you ever leave my life like that again. Promise me that." I said to her as we hugged each other tightly, at the opening of her apartment door.

"I won't leave you; you just make sure you show your behind up here again. Plus, we got a few bachata dances to make up, punk." She said back to me as we laughed together.

"Get out of here. You know you can't see me on that dance floor, punk." I said back as I slightly nudged her right shoulder, then grabbed her and pulled her in close to me to leave a kiss on her forehead. "I'll see you again soon, okay. Be good and take care of the God sent Angel in there. I love you, Mella." I said with a slight pause in the air.

"I want to read our book you're going to write about us one day too. I know it will make best seller but moreover, I know it's going to make me smile. You always do that for me. Be safe out there, see you later, punk." Carmella said with an easy-going smile on her face and slowly shut the door.

After she shut the door, I stood there for a while as I can feel her just looking at me through her peephole, then turned around and went down her stairs and out the front doors. When I was back outside, I looked up and saw Carmella looking out her window, smiling down at me and waving goodbye. That was the very last time I saw Carmella.

Two days after I went to Carmella's new apartment, my homeboy, my cousin and I got into a high-speed car chase with the cops. I had just bought a pound of weed and someone from off the streets just gave me a gun that had a bullet jammed inside it. The person that gave me the gun told me if I could get the bullet out of it, it was my gun to keep. Luckily for me, the gun turned out to be a starter pistol. It was one of those TV blank guns and someone tried to fire a real bullet out of it. So, the gun charge got thrown out in court and they just charged me for the bullet being fired. I was charged for that even though I wasn't the one who actually fired the bullet out of the starter pistol. They ran that concurrent with the pound of weed that I had. I obtained a lawyer for damn near 10-thousand-dollars and he got me a 3-year sentence with a 9-month stipulation. Meaning, I would have to do 3 years in prison if parole never let me out but if I acted right, parole would let me out in 9 months on parole for the remainder of the 3 years. Since I already did 8 months in county jail, going back and forth fighting my case, I would be eligible for parole as soon as I got down state prison. I just wanted to get out of jail already because all I could think about was the woman I had been dating all this time. Her name was Berry and she was Dominican as well. She was the only person there for me besides my mother and sister holding me down heavy and doing this jail time with me. So, I really loved and respected her for that.

My other main concern was of course Carmella. I knew she probably thought I had dissed her. I was so upset with myself because I didn't want her to ever think that I did on purpose. She probably thought I was trying to get her back for standing me up with the college thing or she might have thought I ran away from her because of her new issues in life. I was thinking so many bad things she could have thought as to why she wasn't seeing or hearing from me and I felt so bad. So, I was trying my hardest and fastest to get out of jail.

I went down state hoping the parole board would come and see me within a month's time; but I ended up spending another seven months in prison before the parole board came and released me on parole in June of 2007.

I went looking for Carmella a few times at her new apartment, but she was no longer there. I also tried going to her mother's apartment, but she was no longer there either. I looked up her name on social media and couldn't find her. I tried contacting her through my brother Joe but he was no longer dating Sariah. I was devastated because I felt this time, I had really lost touch with Carmella, forever.

I finally left it alone and moved on with my life. It's 2019 now and I was recently listening to some bachata music and automatically Carmella popped up in my head. I could remember all those good times dancing with her and her family. Memories just started popping up in my head like when I went to court with her for her father's case or the times I used to go pick her up from her job and see her waiting in the parking lot for Lenny to come and get her out of the pouring rain. The time when she stood up for me when I was going to knock Lenny's head off for being racist with me. The time I wrote her a rap love song for her birthday and got her a whole bunch of Winnie the pooh items. Or just simply going to hang with her mother for the day and pop open a few cold Coronas, listening to music while she cooked. All those times just replayed in my mind as I was listening to all those great bachata songs we used to dance to. So, I gave it one more try. I went to go try and find Carmella because all I wanted to tell her was that I got locked up and I didn't mean to let her down when she needed me the most. I wasn't on any revenge stuff with her and I wanted to be there for her; but I couldn't be, due to the fact, I was incarcerated. I wanted to tell her about my life. About my three beautiful children. I moved to Atlanta Georgia in 2010. I wanted to tell her that I knew about her health situation the night I went and saw her and that is why I went. It was to show her that I was still going to be there for her. Still support her through whatever and still genuinely love her. The two main things that I wanted to tell her was, I've always thought about her and I did write that book about her.

Somehow, I came across Sariah's sister's Facebook page. I was super excited when I saw it. I sent a friend request and she immediately accepted. We were always very cool with each other. I think she had a little crush on me herself back in the day; lol but that's beside the point. Jalisa and I connected, conversed and reminisced about the good old days when I used to be around her family heavy. After a two-hour conversation, I finally asked the question. "So, what's been up with your cousin, Carmella?"

She told me that Carmella had been doing well and was just raising her daughter. I asked if she had any social media pages where I could reach out to her; coincidentally, she did. Jalisa said she was on Instagram but her page was private. She gave me Carmella's Instagram name for me to go search for her and told me to send her a friend request and send her a direct message/DM.

I was so excited to hear that Carmella was doing well for herself. After getting the information from Jalisa, I immediately went to search for her and found her. I sent her a friend request and left her a message in her DM. It had been over 10 years since Carmella and I have physically seen one another. I mean, the last time she saw me, I barely even had a mustache on my face and I had hair on my head. I was also about 160 pounds at the time. Fast forward to present day, I have a full beard on my face now, a bald head and I got my weight all the way up. These days I'm weighing in at 195 pounds. I've been in that weight room heavy as well.

I didn't really expect her to know who I was immediately by my pictures alone being that I've physically changed in certain areas that would make me look a lot different. Plus, I wasn't going by my government name on social media. After I found Carmella on Instagram, I also found her mother and her page was open for the public to look at. I was eager to see how Carmella was doing in life. So, I went snooping through her mother's page because I knew she would post about her family. I scrolled down her mother's page and I finally came across a picture with Carmella in it. It was a post about Carmella's birthday. Her caption said how she was so thankful to GOD for having her here to celebrate it with her. Carmella looked happy in the post but I did notice she looked a little different from the last time I had seen her. She was still gorgeous as ever but I could tell life had hit her some as it did for me as well. I knew because I used to study this woman's everything; but all in all, I was just very happy to see her here.

I went to the comment section and left a comment for Carmella. "This day has always been special to me. I used to get you Winnie the Pooh everything on this day. Happy Queen Day Love!!" After leaving that comment on her mother's post I kept scrolling down the page more, just looking for more pictures of Carmella in them. I came across a few of them and just kept seeing this other woman I never seen before in the days I was going to Carmella's family house. This knew woman I kept seeing, started making me wonder a bit because she was in every picture Carmella's mom put up of her, along with Carmella's daughter. I started to wonder was this Carmella's girlfriend or new woman. It would make a lot of sense if she was her woman, considering the other information about what happened to Carmella health wise. I thought all kinds of things when I kept seeing this female in Carmella's picture like maybe when Carmella found out the bad news, she probably started hating men. Maybe the father gave this other woman HIV as well and they joined together to be life partners for Carmella's daughter, Angel. Maybe Carmella had just met this woman randomly and they fell in love with each other. I didn't know; but what I did know was that the last time I saw Carmella, she liked men and now it was looking like she had a whole woman by her side now.

Don't get me wrong…It didn't really matter to me. I still wanted to just get in contact with Carmella and tell her I wrote the book and I would love for her to read it. I also wanted to tell her why I never came back around her apartment and why she hadn't seen me for over a decade.

Weeks went by and I would check every day to see if she responded to my comment; but she never responded. I also checked the DM and friend request I sent to her; but she never accepted and never messaged me back in the DM. I was losing hope again. I often wondered if she knew it was me or if she even saw the message. I was losing hope, but I didn't give up. I was born a champion and I was always taught that if you want something so badly, you have to keep pushing towards your goal of getting it. So, I tried another route.

One day, I inboxed Sariah on Facebook after reconnecting with her and told her to tell her cousin Carmella that I've been DMing her and to check it. Sariah said she would do that for me and 10 seconds later, I got a DM back from Carmella.

"HEY!! How you been? What's up with you?"

It was the day of Carmella birthday April 9th, 2019. I was super excited she had responded back!! I said to myself, *we have a Pulse!!* I immediately messaged her back and told her I didn't expect for her to hold a long conversation with me because I knew she was celebrating her birthday; but that I was so glad to be reconnected and we had to catch up. I waited and waited and waited for an "Ok" or some type of response back; but I never got it.

I was cool with that though because at least she knew who I was now and could always go on my Instagram page and see how I was doing in life; she could always get in contact with me in the DM if need be. I could always go on her mother's page and see pictures of time passed. I will forever cherish the memories and love I had for this beautiful woman named Carmella. I am satisfied now that she is good in life and at peace. I wanted to complete the very last thing I ever told her I was going to do and that's write this book. After not responding back to me, I decided to no longer be in pursuit of Carmella and I wish her nothing but the best in life. That would just have to be enough for me and I except it because frankly, she seems satisfied and at peace with being the crush that crushed me.

The End.

"This story was written with many lessons in mind. The first, to be bold in love. It's a clear example of how you'll miss 100% of the shots you never take, but missing the ones you do take is not the end of the world. It's also a lesson in letting go; but the main lesson is this...Live your life to the fullest with no regrets; but always try to be safe in whatever it is you're doing. I say "try" because mistakes are a part of growing; we all have made some. Just try not to repeat those same mistakes twice; learn your lesson the first time around. Most importantly, do everything you can to reach your highest potential because you never know how much time you actually have. Life will be what you make it. Enjoy all of its beautiful moments, thank God every day, and stay focused; because if life catches you slipping...eventually, it all comes crashing down on you. Piece by piece until you're completely CRUSHED." - STOCKY BONZZ

Made in the USA
Columbia, SC
23 May 2021